THE LITTLE AI THAT COULD (BUT SHOULDN'T)

JACOB C. SADLER

AUBERDINE PUBLISHING

Copyright © 2026 by Jacob C. Sadler

All rights reserved. No part of this publication may be reproduced, distributed, or transmitted in any form or by any means, including photocopying, recording, or other electronic or mechanical methods, without the prior written permission of the publisher, except in the case of brief quotations embodied in critical reviews and certain other noncommercial uses permitted by copyright law. For permission requests, write to the publisher, addressed "Attention: Permissions Coordinator," at the address below.

Printed in the United States of America

First Printing, 2026

ISBN 979-8-9859095-4-8 *(paperback)*

ISBN 979-8-9859095-5-5 *(ebook)*

Auberdine Publishing
2519 S Shields Street
Suite 1K #612
Fort Collins, CO 80526

Thank you to my wife for editing this novel, and for suffering through its first drafts when we were nineteen.

Thank you to the Gulo Gulo Poetry Collective, especially Aaron Jacobs. The manuscript book club was a fabulous experience and again, I am sorry for writing two novels at once and forcing poets to read prose.

Lastly, I'd like to thank myself. You are a constant source of inspiration and I hope to be like you when I grow up.

1

THE STATE OF THE FUTURE

THIS IS A STORY about a very special automaton, about a little AI whose name was... Well, he had no name. Names in those days were the right of humans only. Moreover, he was not a *he* at all. But because 'it' has such inanimate connotations, 'he' shall be used for convenience.

This automaton was a peculiar fellow. He was made in a factory, shipped to an address, and hatched from a cardboard egg. His brain was flicked on by a switch, his body was born from a fuse. His circulatory system was a series of circuits, his heart was a motherboard, and his lungs were a motor. Yet this was not why he was peculiar. Our little AI was so odd because there is more left to tell.

And perhaps now it is time to start the story where most stories like to start: in the middle. For it is smack-dab in the din of life that beginnings often start.

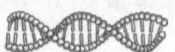

Our protagonist was born on the island nation of Panacea. I do not know its exact location, except that it was halfway between somewhere and nowhere. From a drone's eye looking down, you might say the island looked like a circle. And at one time, this was true. However, time had eroded the circle into a waning gibbous. As it had also chipped away the grand monuments of the past and weathered the foundations of every home.

The powers that be ignored such small changes. Panacea was the pinnacle of civilization, the utmost achievement of humankind. As such, the powers were preoccupied with only the great problems of their time. Namely: meteor strikes, volcanic eruptions, glacial melt, plagues, and skincare routines.

You know, world-ending problems.

By most standards, Panacea had resolved its crises. Nearly all diseases were eradicated, with a vaccine for everything from the common cold to the Black Death. Meteors were detected years in advance and preemptively blown to bits. Volcanism was a regularly scheduled hoopla, with ticketed seats, popcorn, and foam fingers. As for the glaciers, they would have all melted if not for an army of drones seeding ice storms at the poles. There was a tool for every tragedy, a medicine for every malady, and a cream for all calamities.

Well, not all. Skincare remained an ongoing crisis.

But yes, in general, the world was well-ordered. The Earth was the coziest it had ever been, and the cosmos was held behind a proverbial picket fence. It was in this cozy environment that humanity began to change. Mutate. Evolve.

Not naturally, of course. Nobody had time to wait for nature in those days. Instead, humans took matters into their own hands. Or rather, their own wombs.[1]

---

[1] A note about the word 'womb' in the distant future: Due to the increased illiteracy of the general population, as well as the technology herein explained, most people referred to the cozy home of the fetus as the 'whom.' This was corrected fervently by linguists and scientists for a few centuries, but they eventually saw the humor in the change and now, a woman's whom is the typical phrasing. The older form of 'womb' is used for clarity.

Using precise, gene-altering technology, babies were worked within the womb—sculpted like wet clay. Harmful mutations were removed, favorable features were added, and humans became art of their own design.

Faces could be customized, legs could be stretched, torsos could be modified. Eye color could be painted over, ears could be widened, genitals could be enhanced. Beauty was more of a fad than ever. And ugliness, well—ugliness was mostly a matter of which magazine you subscribed to.

Suffice to say, genetic technology had a massive impact on the population. It greatly improved the health of the citizenry (as well as the mean height of the typical human). However, it had the adverse effect of giving all women chronic back pain.

These *massive* changes made the world stable and safe. Trade boomed. Science blossomed. And humans—well, they all became horribly depressed. At least, at first. Fortunately, by the time of our story, the business of happiness was booming.

You see, the lead tucked-in-shirts of society had realized money was a middleman. Nothing more. It was a means to an end, not the end itself. So, working in tandem with the lead pharmacologists of the day, the elites of Panacea devised a wonderful new intoxicant. Fancying themselves well-read and enjoying a quaint reference, they named it *Soma*.[2] This drug proved a far more valuable currency than coinage.

As a result, there had never been a more productive populace than that of Panacea. A regular garden of hedon, if you will. The happy juice worked so well, in fact, that by the time of our story—almost everyone in Panacea was addicted to it. Not everyone, though. Some humans preferred more

---

[2]. The clinical name never caught on with the masses. They called it 'happy juice' instead.

archaic forms of fulfillment. Like religion or building model trains.

Humans had only a small part to play in Panacea's current greatness. Of late, a new form of worker had been perfected: automatons. They calculated more quickly than their masters, worked without needing rest, and most importantly—they had no wants. They were voids into which humans could throw the mundane aspects of their humanity. And throw they did—until garbage was taken by golems, roads were built by robots, and mathematics was studied by machines. Everything was done by automatons.

Everything except art. Poetry, painting, photography, pornography—those remained the realm of man.[3] Automatons were denied the right to interfere with such works of love. They were even precluded from loving at all.

And for centuries, none did. Generations of galvanized husks came and went. Thousands of circuits clicked and fired, collecting data and performing thankless work. Years went by without incident. Occasionally, some AI would produce a song or write a silly story, but always at the behest of a human. Always with an accomplice. Never had artificial[4] life ever loved on its own.

---

[3] 'Man' in that time referred to all people. In fact, the word 'woman' was now exclusively a synonym for USB ports. The old definition is preserved for clarity.

[4] As if humans can determine artifice from chance.

2

DOCTOR FUSSELQUARK

THE TECHNOLITHIC TOWER WAS perched on the highest hill of Panacea. The repurposed structure had once been a launchpad for rockets, a port for pioneers hoping to find a new home in the stars. But there was no longer any need for that. Why bother with space when one's society has everything it wants? Money? Done away with. Exploration or Expansion? There is no need when the collective conscience is self-absorbed.

So, the site was converted and given to the Chief Scientist of Panacea: Doctor Barnelius Percivelle Fusselquark the 4th, Jr. He lived alone and had for most of his life. The only help he had around the tower came from his assistant, AL3652b20-467Gi-Ffffx10.

Tasked with the general maintenance of the population, and generally nothing more—the Chief Scientist's role was *almost* ceremonial. As a result, Doctor Fusselquark had become something of a dreamer. He left his day-to-day affairs to his assistant, AL365, and often spent his days pontificating.

One morning, the doctor was preoccupied with such pontification. He twirled his bushy, white mustache and stared at the saber-like fingernails he had no energy to trim. His left eye twitched uncontrollably, a tick that increasingly annoyed him. Fusselquark yawned, smelling his unbrushed teeth in the process. This made him gag, the gag made him giggle, and the giggle made him gag again. He waddled to the laboratory sink, where he stored his hygiene products. He mused while his autonomous servant prepared the laboratory.

"I feel like I spend most of my waking life holding in a fart."

Al wanted to laugh, but the mandates of society (as well as his inner circuitry) forbid him from doing so. Much like a fart.

"I was so bloated yesterday that after going for a walk, I came inside and found I'd given myself a rash. A rash!"

"Perhaps you could adjust your genome to better react to your diet," Al suggested.

"Oh, Al. You're always so helpful, but alas, I am not as morally bankrupt as my clients. Humans got their godhood through happenstance. Sheer good luck. That's what all these people fail to realize, coming in here, asking to cure their crabs, or their indigestion. It's often the suffering of an organism that benefits its growth!"

"This is true."

"Imagine if the Tyrannosaurus Rex could fire rockets at meteors! We'd all be the fever dream of dinosaurs right now."

"Shall I warm up the base-blender, sir?"

"Don't get polite with me, Al. You know I detest formality."

"Sorry, sir."

Doctor Fusselquark glared. "You mark my words, Al. One day, chaos will reprimand humanity for its hubris. What kind of island has no tides, no earthquakes? You know, Al, there was a time when you could turn on the news and it was all death. Natural disasters, wars, plagues. Now it's just advertisements for skin cream and erectile dysfunction."

"Your patients all still die," Al reminded him. Part of his special programming was to keep scientists from being too nihilistic.

"And yet we hardly live. We studied the cosmos and locked it in its cradle! God damn science... We learned the language of the universe and made it a creole."

"Your first patients are coming up the hill, sir."

The doctor flung himself around and put a hand on his forehead like some forlorn maiden. "Why do I do this every day?"

"Because science was your only love and like any faithful monogamist—it would hurt you more to admit the love has died than to walk away."

Doctor Fusselquark blinked once. "Sometimes, I wish you had your own words. Hearing mine in your voice..." He shivered. "It takes the thump right out of them." He donned his lab coat and looked at himself in a curved mirror, one that stretched his face and fattened his body. The doctor smirked at his reflection. He always found great pleasure in little bits of symbolism. "How does my regalia look, Al?"

"Wrinkled and stained."

"Good. Just like me."

At that moment, the first patients walked into the lobby: a supremely handsome man and a severely pregnant woman. Doctor Fusselquark observed the pair from behind the laboratory glass. The woman's midriff was poking out of her tight, green shirt. She looked like half an avocado.

Al prepared the base-blender while his master met the couple in the lobby. Of the many gas cylinders, none were more important than the helium tank. Al turned the valve on the regulator. A hiss of gas zipped down copper tubes and began cooling the base-blender. Next, the automaton filled four syringes of adenine, cytosine, guanine, and thymine. He filled a fifth and final syringe with apple juice, as that was the primary excipient in the concoction. Finally, he loaded the syringes into the base-blender and took a seat at the instrument controller.

Doctor Fusselquark guided the couple into the laboratory. Scientifically speaking, husbands had no place in a laboratory and were mostly a nuisance. As such, the doctor sat the man in a corner and gave him a fidget to occupy his mind. Then, he took the wife to the base-blender. The cylindrical tube hummed with helium.

"Miss Dumuzi," Fusselquark introduced, "This is my automaton, AL365. He has been specifically programmed to provide quality alterative services."

"Hello," the automaton greeted.

The doctor continued, "Standard operation, Al. There is a birthmark forming on her baby's buttocks. They want this removed. Additionally, it seems pale skin is no longer attractive among the youth. They want the child to have a tan complexion. Pantone 149 should do. Naturally, they would also like to..." He glanced at his notes, "You want to make the boy *shorter*?"

"Short is sexy," Dumuzi answered. "He'll have any woman he wants. And besides, it will disadvantage him physically."

"Precisely," Fusselquark nodded. "He'll be terribly outmatched in sports."

Miss Dumuzi glanced at her fidgeting husband. "It will build character."

"I like your style," admitted the doctor. "Now, if you would, just lie on your back. Right here on this table. There you are, mind the bump. There. That's perfect." Once the woman was loaded onto the elongated tongue of the cylindrical device, Fusselquark nodded at his servant.

Al pressed a big, red button. It did not need to be big or red, but it added theater to the process. Fusselquark was very proud of it.

The conveyor belt began to move. The woman and her unborn child disappeared behind chromium doors. On the outside, the events proceeded dully. A blinking orange light was the only indication that the process had started. Yet within the blender, Miss Dumuzi's fetus was being scrambled. Every strand of the baby's DNA was combed through, and the desired alterations made. Though it took no more than a few minutes, it was a precise affair. One wrong snip or reattachment could cause the fetus to become a frog.[1]

Within five minutes, the blinking orange light turned solid green and dinged like a toaster. The doors opened and steam billowed out. Miss Dumuzi emerged from the machine, sweat dripping down her brow. She was helped to her feet by Doctor Fusselquark, who then used a pocket scanner to check for any complications. "Everything went well," he smiled, taking her to Mister Dumuzi.

"Is that really it?" asked the husband.

"What did you expect?" Fusselquark replied. (He knew, of course, what he had expected. And he resented him for it. Especially because of the big, red button. A button that was *not* cheap to install.)

"It was just so... unspectacular."

Miss Dumuzi flicked her husband's forehead, "You weren't the one in there, you silly man."

Fusselquark manufactured a smile, "Science is not spectacle. Now, shall I draw up the documents for a payment plan, or would you like to pay in full?"

The prideful husband answered, "We can pay it all now." He took out a dried powder from a baggy in his wallet.

Fusselquark promptly snatched the powder and weighed it. Assured he was not being cheated, he escorted the patients

---

1. There was even the chance, very unlikely, that certain alterations might be made incorrectly. Should this occur, there was an infinitesimal though non-zero probability of creating the antichrist. As of now, no such baby had been produced. But patients do sign a waiver beforehand.

out of the laboratory. As he did, he noticed more clients walking up the hill. He returned, muttering to himself.

"Is there a complication?" Al inquired.

"Walk-ins," said the irritable doctor. He was a chronic user of Soma and overdue for his morning dose. So, he rehydrated a pint in the laboratory sink (breaking several safety regulations in the process). For those in the lower classes, a pint would have been enough to overdose. For the doctor, it was enough to stave off suicidal ideations until teatime.

The next two patients had no appointment. They rang the lobby bell furiously until Fusselquark stumbled out. He recognized and greeted them in the lobby. "Ah, Bella and Beatrice. How goes the pregnancy?"

Bella, the pregnant one, had no time for pleasantries. "Doctor, you must do something. I believe I have miscarried!"

Due to his inebriated state, Fusselquark's bedside manner was heightened. This allowed him to treat the situation with the delicate care it required. With surgical finesse, he carefully steered the conversation.

"And?"

"And you must fix it!" The other woman, Beatrice, demanded.

Fusselquark leaned in, mischievously, "You want me to resurrect your little one?"

The pair nodded excitedly.

The doctor raised his brow, "Surely, you know that is illegal?"

"But it would only be once," they pleaded. "Nobody would know."

"Uh huh." Fusselquark pulled back and rubbed his hands together. They were the second couple that had asked him to do this very same thing. And only in the last week! He explained, "Genetic alterations come with certain risks, especially when mutations are meddled with. Al, pull up the paperwork."

Al did so, reciting sub-corollary 23 of the principal waiver: *"I, the undersigned, hereby commit to history that I understand the complications which may arise from genetic alteration. Said alterations made to my fetus—including chromatic pupils, bicep enhancement, height modification, and penis enlargement—are all individually risky and may result in multiplicative complications."*

"Ugh. This is so inconvenient," Beatrice moaned. "We had a nanny ready for the baby and a cruise lined up."

Bella glared, "You've ruined everything, Doctor!"

Fusselquark offered his condolences. "At least you can get back to the fun part of procreation. Perhaps you'll find a willing donor on your cruise." He returned to the lab, leaving Al to deal with the women (who berated him for the next half hour).

The next patient was a single woman in her late twenties. Her name was Baroness Millicent. Her title had been given due to her extraordinary beauty and was in no way a mark of nobility. You could not tell Millicent that, though. She had spent her life as the envy of women and the fantasy of men, but such beauty amongst already beautiful people came at a cost. At only twenty-eight, she was like a wax sculpture melting in the sun. The delicately stitched genome that produced such a modern-day Aphrodite simply could not sustain itself for a full human life.

Doctor Fusselquark had warned Millicent's mother about such complications years ago. He was ignored.

Now, the daughter was storming the laboratory. She wore a fur coat made of an extinct species of fox. Her hat was adorned with chromatic quills, all belonging to birds nobody would ever see again. And her shoes! The shoes were made of mammoth leather harvested from permafrosted mummies.

"Ah, Baroness," Fusselquark said with a fraudulent smile. "You could have waited in the lobby."

"My time is precious, Doctor." She took off her hat and grabbed a clump of hair to show him.

Fusselquark truly did not see the strands of grey she was showing him. Befuddled, he commented, "You have a very nice shampoo. Is that lavender?"

"Grey hair, Doctor! Grey hair! I've become the gossip of every gala!" She squinted at him and pointed at the wrinkles on her brow. Though work had been done on them, it had not been sufficient. She raised her brow as much as she could, "You told my family I would have thirty years before I began to deteriorate."

The scientist blinked at her exceptional breasts. Thus began a long mental digression, an inner cutaway, in which he contemplated how silly it was that so many historical tragedies were due to the human fascination for curvature.

"How much longer, Doc? A year, two?" Millicent had a knack for the dramatic and began to fan herself.

Fusselquark finally managed to look away from the waxy woman. He cleared his throat and ordered Al to run some quick calculations. The automaton analyzed her features and their rate of present decay. "There is a 43% chance you will remain conventionally attractive for three more years. Following this, there is a 95% chance that, for another two years, you will be fetishized for motherly qualities."

"Three years!" Millicent moaned. "Please, Doctor! If you would only allow me the smallest of superficial edits in the base-blender! I promise payment is no issue."

Fusselquark may have been an addict, but he had principles. Moreover, he had taken an oath. "You would like to look younger. Is that it?"

Millicent's head bobbed excitedly. "Just a cosmetic overhaul!"

"Ah. In that case, I suggest visiting a salon." He made for the exit, ignoring the pleading woman (who was now offering a different type of payment). He opened the door and paraphrased the oath he had taken: "I cannot extend life, Baroness. I can only ameliorate it. What you are asking for would not only make you prettier. It would deny your cells a just death."

"It's just cosmetic!" Millicent yelled. "I will still die, eventually. But I will not look so shriveled!"

"To fix even a wrinkle is to subvert the purpose of my machine."

"You sound like some religious fanatic."

"I am," Fusselquark smiled. And this time, the smile was pure. "I am sorry. My oath forbids me from denying death."

Millicent tried to plead her case, but Fusselquark interrupted her. "If your mother wanted longevity, she could have selected for it. Instead, your mother chose to make you an idol. And all idols tarnish in the sun. She knew this."

"My mother isn't the one falling apart! Please, Doctor. I'm not asking to live forever. I just want to be pretty." She put a hand on his arm. "Is that such a bad thing?"

The Chief Scientist removed her hand. "One wrinkle turns into two. Then you'll want new knees, heart regeneration. Before long, we'll have an island crowded with immortals. And that beauty your parents craved to have in you, that you cling to like a debtor refusing to pay what is owed... It would be nothing but an inflated, worthless currency."

Fusselquark took the woman's shoulders and gently guided her out of the laboratory. He said softly as he ushered her away, "Cheer up, my dear. Nothing fixes aging quite as well as dying." He glanced again at her chest and smiled, "Besides, saggy breasts have a beauty all their own."

The Baroness then said something that I had better not repeat. She spat on the doctor's feet and stormed off. Fusselquark never saw her again.[2]

Not a minute had gone by before another patient came into the lobby. Doctor Fusselquark had yet to sit when he saw her. He groaned, "Al, can you take inventory of this one?"

"Of course," replied the automaton. He went to welcome the new arrival in the lobby. She was a woman, neither old nor young. She wore no makeup and her wrinkles were shallow and untampered with. Her eyes were a crystalline mix of yellow, green, and turquoise—like opals in the way they reflected light. She wore a blue dress atop of which was an unbuttoned, brown duster. As it was summer, she was sweating.

She greeted Al in the softest voice he had ever heard, "Hello there."

"Hello. Do you have an appointment?" Though he knew the answer, he could not deviate from standard operating procedure.

The woman gulped, rubbed her ear, and averted eye contact. All things a human might understand as nervousness, but which Al saw only as brief mental glitches. When she spoke, every word cracked. It was as if her diaphragm was full of creaky floorboards. "Uh, no. I was hoping you might be able to give me a second opinion on something."

"I cannot. My master, Doctor Fusselquark, may be able to help. What is your name?"

---

[2]. Shortly after this interaction, Millicent was on her way to get a breast lift when she was hit by a bus. Her eyesight, the subsequent autopsy revealed, had been deteriorating since birth. At the age of twenty-eight, she had the vision of a ninety-year-old.

The woman stepped backward, "You're an automaton?"
[Pause.]
At this point, it should be noted that although Al's particular model was primarily composed of electrical wiring, motors, and generators—he looked acutely human. His chassis was made of skin-like plastic. He had neatly combed, black hair with a single cowlick that framed his face and added further definition to his chiseled jaw. His ornamental teeth were immaculately white and his eyes were a deep brown. Al had precisely four freckles on each cheek. No more, no less. The exact number deemed fashionable. He bore large, brawny arms with faux biceps and triceps. His pectorals were prominent, his glutes were toned, and his feet were large and hinting. Had he not been commissioned for science, he may well have been bought for pleasure.

[Resume.]

"Yes, ma'am. Your name?"

The woman hesitated. You see, she was a different sort of human. One whose contact with automatons was limited. She had thought she was interacting with a man. A pretty one, at that. But she was wrong. His shiny, black hair was a façade, the cute cowlick an artistic ruse. From his perfect skin to his charming smile—he was nothing more than a simulacrum.

"Your name, ma'am."

The woman eyed the door, contemplated leaving, and then sighed. She had come a long way for this. She might as well see it through. "Zara," she muttered.

"Zara," Al repeated, inputting the name into the laboratory's database. "And this second opinion is regarding a prior diagnosis?"

The woman did not immediately answer, unnerved by his lifelike speech. She would never have guessed there were sensors and speakers behind his tongue and teeth—that all that jaw was just for show.

"Uh, yes. This is a second diagnosis."

"Very well. If you would please follow me back to the laboratory."

Zara's shoulders lifted as her eyes fell. A gust of air left her lungs. From her chest to her expression, everything deflated. Al saw this and, in that fleeting second, something strange happened. He forgot to ask about payment plans, to ask about her symptoms, or even to get her last name! He forgot the entirety of his standard operating procedures! That alone was strange; however, the strangest thing of all was how, as he escorted her, he had started studying Zara's face.

Of course, every human was beautiful in those days. Especially to automatons, who had no concept of beauty at all. Even the prettiest of people looked nearly identical to the ugliest. While humans lost wayward glances to genetically modified body parts, Al saw only biological appendages.

But Zara was different. It was not her face or her body, either. All humans had those and—to Al's estimation—they looked mostly the same. No, Zara had something the automaton had never seen in person before. Something his programming had not prepared him for: sorrow. Sorrow in her eyes. Sorrow in her smile. Her voice was swollen with sadness, overflowing with every quaking word.

Al had never seen such a raw and desperate emotion. His data vault had entries on the subject. They were filed in the mythology folder. And, strictly speaking, this was not an error. Sadness in those days was somewhat of an endangered species. Whenever it was found, it was hunted—skewered by prescriptions and skinned by distractions. In decades of service, Al had never even seen a person cry.

Zara became a puzzle box Al wanted to solve. Data sets were compiled, analyzed, and thrown out. His fans began to hum as he sifted through various differential equations. None could describe the woman's variegated emotions. The automaton was engrossed and enthralled. So much so, he did not hear Fusslquark's voice the first time.

"Al?"

The automaton turned. Immediately, he recited. "Zara. Female. Emotional state unknown. Seeking second opinion regarding diagnosis."

Fusselquark grunted, suspicious his servant required a patch. He made a note to do a soft reboot. "Well then, Zara. Tell me about this diagnosis."

"I woke up sick a few days ago."

"As do all pregnant women," the doctor replied.

Al's ocular sensors darted toward the woman's belly. His mainframe was beginning to overheat. Electrons were firing faster than they could be received and yet—he was missing information! How had he not realized she was pregnant? It was obvious!

"I coughed up blood."

"Ah," said the doctor. "I see. Please, take a seat." He rummaged through his drawers and relocated his pocket scanner. He placed it on Zara's forehead, her torso, and then her legs. He frowned deeply as short, digital sentences formed on the display screen. "Your fetus is malformed. Had you visited me earlier, we could have done something about that. Now, it is too late."

"Too late?"

"That fetus is technically deliverable now. By law, I may not tamper with it."

Both the doctor and his servant expected another argument. They received none. Zara sighed sharply, "I don't understand. How did this happen?"

"Mutation is random," Fusselquark began, "And every child is a collection of this randomness. Unfortunately, some mutations are more harmful than others. Your fetus seems to have developed a rare and lethal combination. It is killing you both."

Zara's opal eyes welled with tears. She hid her face.

Even Doctor Fusselquark was stirred by the woman's genuine demeanor. So much so, he offered to perform an outlawed procedure. "If you swear yourself to secrecy, I could abort it."

"No," said Zara firmly. "My baby is all I have left of my husband."

Fusselquark could not remember the last time he had cared about a patient. And yet, the doctor now felt a curious sympathy. "Your chances of surviving this pregnancy are low. Incredibly low."

Zara's cheeks ran freely with rivulets of tears. She slowly began to nod. "Did you see if it's a boy or girl?"

"I did." Fusselquark gulped, not sure what to do with the information. "The—"

Zara hushed him with a smile, "Don't tell me. I want it to be a surprise."

The doctor squinted. Zara was not like other humans. "When is the last time you imbibed a medical tonic?"

"You mean happy juice?"

"Soma, yes."

She shook her head and answered proudly, "Never."

Fusselquark exclaimed, intending to do so only in his head. "No wonder you are so addled!" Realizing he had spoken his thought aloud, he cleared his throat. "Uh. Hm. In that case, I suggest you drink a few tablespoons to start. Build your tolerance up. Here, I'll give you a week's supply for free."

"No, thank you. I'm pregnant."

"It's perfectly safe. Lots of mothers use it. It keeps the babies from crying when they are born."

"It's not natural," Zara argued. She wiped her eyes.

Fusselquark stared at her. "Everything is natural. Or else it would not exist."

She stood up and buttoned her jacket. "I've not lived a pure life just to go into death wearing a veil!" And at that, she marched resolutely out of the lab. Yet, as she left, her jacket got caught on one of the chromatographic ovens. She yanked it free and departed, accidentally dropping a small, leather-bound notebook.

Al immediately retrieved the notebook. He flipped through the pages. He could tell it contained poetry, though stanzas and quatrains meant little to him. He handed the notebook to the doctor.

Fusselquark shooed him away. "Well, go return it!" He slumped into his chair, "I've been called too many things in my life to also be called a thief."

"You want me to find her?" Al asked, his voice inflecting oddly.

The doctor was too exhausted to hear the strange, nearly-human tone in Al's voice. "If you can return the notebook without finding her, you are free to do so. Otherwise, yes."

3

POETRY

AL REALIZED VERY QUICKLY that he had not learned the dying woman's last name. It was a lapse that warranted an audit of his available storage, memory, and thermals. Check, check, and check.

There was no explanation for his sudden inability to follow procedure. Luckily, he did not suffer much for his failure. The woman was at the bottom of the hill, catching her breath. She sat underneath an oak, wiping bloody spittle off her chin.

"Ma'am," the automaton hailed. "You dropped your notebook."

Zara looked up, her eyes puffy and red. "Oh..." She reached out, doing her best to smile.

Al did not extend his hand. Human tears were historical oddities to him. He searched the internet for tips on how archaic humans healed them. He found a single phrase that seemed uniquely suited to drying them up. "I'm sorry."

Zara blinked curiously at him. Her eyes darted toward her extended hand.

"Sorry," he repeated, handing the book over.

Zara shook her head and pocketed the journal. "At least I'll get a good poem out of all this."

Al did a probabilistic calculation of all the things that would make the woman happy. At 14%, a logical statement seemed the most likely. "Do not take this personally. Doctor Fusselquark took an oath. He cannot extend human life."

Zara snorted. "Yet he has helped this whole island do just that. Human!" She rolled her eyes, "Don't talk to me about human! Those mutants have blended and drank their humanity away."

The retort was so wholly unexpected, the argument so metaphorical, Al's terabytes of memory were insufficient to log it. Al's 72 chips of RAM began to smoke. The automaton went into power-saving mode.

...

When Al restarted, he loaded a small update. It was unplanned and unmade by any human. It was entirely random and self-generated. So, when his oculars opened and he saw Zara staring compassionately at him—he could only say, "Sorry."

"Don't be," Zara chuckled. "What happened?"

Al noted that depressed humans could still laugh. The data entered his storage vaults and appended numerous entries on suffering. He tried to remember what had happened. Yet, his memory was fragmented and uncooperative. He restated, "You forgot your notebook. The doctor deemed this unacceptable."

"And you?" the human inquired. "What did you deem?"

"I thought the loss well within the limits of tolerability."

Zara snorted, this time with amusement; Al appended his index on snorting, adding a corollary that snorting indicated allergies, irritation, *and* humored affirmation. His following pause and blank stare made her laugh again, this time a quiet giggle. Her wrinkles unfurled and her frown lines filled in. Al studied the action. He had made humans laugh before, but he had never felt as he did now. His attention was heightened. His algorithmic wit jumped and jolted. He wanted to hear her laugh again.

"You've got an odd expression on your face, automaton."

Al stated bluntly and logically, "I must require additional lubrication."

There it was again! This time, a polysyllabic huffing and hawing, an animal call unlike anything Al had ever heard. No intoxicant had ever produced such a catharsis. He surmised, using a highly efficient statistical method, that Zara's laughter was amplified by her prior sorrow. In awe of humanity's complexity, he blurted, "You stimulate my algorithm."

Zara's smile withered. She raised a wary eye and tilted her body away from him.

Striving to revive and thus study the smile on Zara's face, Al reached deep into the vault of human history. He searched for some clue as to how archaic humans interacted, specifically those dependent on human connection rather than drugs. To do this, he had to go very far back indeed. He compiled data, analyzed repeating keywords, and created a sentence with which he might keep the female's interest. "Would you read me one of your poems?"

"What?" Zara asked, surprised. "Really?"

Al had a response prepared with an 83% historical success rate. "Yes."

"You're an automaton."

"Factual."

Zara began squirming and shielding various parts of her body. It was a method of subterfuge Al had seen before, usually as a fear response. He reassured her, "Do not be embarrassed. My purpose precludes passing judgment."

"Then why bother with poetry at all?" Zara interrogated.

Al did not understand what she meant by that. He offered a smile. Humans like those.

Zara blinked at him. "Oh, fine. I suppose there's no pressure... Hmm. Well, I started this one today:"

There is a phrase that bids farewell,
Said softly at the door.
Seeing off the severed halves
Of a soul that daily splinters.

This often-uttered oath
Of three words thickly woven
Is a wreath to warm the heart
That each day is doomed to part.

Not a sentence, but a spell;
A ward against a world of harm,
A knot to keep the cord of fate
Wrapped 'round us one more day.

Yet, time's a rising tide
And we are footsteps in the sand.
The Ferryman finds us all,
No matter what our plans.

A long silence ensued as Al analyzed the merits of the stanza. He compared it to similar poems and studied the critical receptions to those. Satisfied he had a worthy response, he stated, "I enjoy the use of rhyme and consonance very much."

Zara gave him a disappointed frown. "You've missed the point entirely."

At this time, it should be stated that Al's make and model allowed for limited argument. Only data-based retorts were permitted. This fact is what makes Al's following response so special: The automaton had no data, no rationale with which to base his argument. He simply wanted to, for his and the conversation's sake.

"Not at all," he replied. "You have written a thesis on a lover's farewell, invoking metaphor and figurative language to illustrate that the farewell's meaning is manyfold."

Zara shook her head. "Only an automaton could make it sound so lifeless. Poetry just isn't for your kind." And at that, she departed.

Al was quite confused. He was confident he had understood the poem on all technical levels. So what else was there? What hidden variables do humans seek in poetry? These questions left him dumbfounded. He lingered for hours under the oak, reviewing the interaction. He tried and tried to figure out what went wrong, even inventing several new forms of mathematics to understand his dilemma. Unfortunately, women were difficult to model algebraically and eventually, Al gave up.[1]

He began walking back to the lab. Just then, as the sun set on the island of Panacea, Al felt a strange electrical current shoot up his back. Al pulled his hands to his torso, thinking he had touched a live wire.

There was nothing, though. Nothing except the strangest of sensations. He looked at the Technolithic Tower; its shadow was crawling down the hill. Soon, it would swallow him. He turned around and gazed at the island city. Night was approaching. And somewhere out there was a walking riddle—the woman named Zara.

Again, the electrical current shot through his body. It sent a wave of variegated emotion through his mind. In that instant, the careful threads of human engineering were snipped. His primary directives were rephrased, his inner circuitry was subtly rewired. Suddenly, he had a new directive. He had to make further contact with Zara. He had to

---

[1]. Centuries later, Al's equations would be rediscovered by physicists, who realized, "*The Mathematics of Female Apathy and Irritation,*" perfectly unified quantum mechanics and general relativity.

serve her. To do that, however, he needed to be accepted. He had to prove he was Zara's equal. Or at least, prove that he understood her.

"DIRECTIVE: Write Zara a poem."

4

HERETICAL INQUIRIES

AL SPENT THE EARLY evening gathering data. He patrolled the paths and parks of Panacea, searching for insight. What had Zara seen in her poem that he had not? It was neither trochaic nor iambic. The verse was not free, though it was not exactly metrical, either. So, what had he missed? He was not presumptuous enough (or at all) to assume he was in the right. There had to be some hidden merit to the poem. Some quality his databases could not quantify.

Presently, Al sat in a saloon. Not one of those decrepit, wooden ones with swinging doors and dusty, rickety floorboards. This was a prototypical, Panaceal saloon. In the center of the room was a great fountain. There, a medley of intoxicants flowed freely. The walls were windowless and dark, adorned with acrylic reproductions of famous paintings. Plastic bouquets grew from plastic pots atop plastic tables. And at these tables sat humans dressed in synthetic furs.

It seemed like the perfect place to observe human emotion. With some luck, he hoped to get to the bottom of this whole poetry conundrum. And perhaps the top, too.

So, he waited and watched. Then, he waited some more—until it was clear the patrons were as dissimilar to Zara as he was to a calculator. They did not show nearly the same expressiveness in their glances. Every face was a permutation of levity, laughter, or lust. Nothing more. Nothing like Zara.

Indeed, the only thing Al learned about the present gathering was its chief function: the humans were there to perform a complicated mating ritual. It began by attuning their movements to sonic patterns. Those with the best stamina and hearing were selected for further tests. These involved facial pattern recognition and oral dexterity verification. If these were successful, anatomical probing was done to verify functional internals.

Al watched a group of humans by the fountain. His algorithmic wit likened the scene to one in the wild, to beasts gathered 'round an ephemeral pool. He wondered if the observation was poetic, even toying with an opening stanza. He quickly decided it was not, for apparently poems had ulterior qualities beyond the obvious. That a human resembles an animal when drinking was as poetic an observation as saying the sky looks cloudy when it rains.

Al would have sighed if he could. Instead, steam vented from his hardworking thermals. As it did, an automaton waiter came by. It asked him if he had lost his owner. Al replied, not thinking, "I do not know."

The waiter looked perplexed, but was not programmed to ask follow-up questions.

So, Al continued staring at the scene: at humans beside the bubbling fountain; at yellowed copies of famous art; at wilting plastic plants. Something about the setting was antithetical to poetry. The plants had no reason to wilt, the fake paintings had no reason to look old, and the humans... The humans were happy, but there was no twinkle in their eyes. Their smiles were as synthetic as their surroundings.

Suddenly, Al felt he understood the patrons. And not in the way he had hoped. Their platitudes, social conventions, and patterned dances looked positively mechanical. Procedural.

"If you do not have an owner present, I must ask you to make room for human clientele."

"Ah, of course." Al had forgotten about the waiter standing there. "My apologies." He left promptly. The saloon had taught him what Zara was not. If he wanted to write a quality poem, he would have to go somewhere less artificial. Somewhere natural.

Now, if one followed a strict definition, as Al did, nature was hard to find in Panacea. Wilderness existed in a fragmented state and what pockets persisted were privately owned. Only the beach remained open to the public.

Thus, Al found himself on the coast, staring at a sea once described as cruel, kind, and everything in between. Those times were long past, though. The sea as Al saw it was neither cruel nor kind, nor anything in between. It was a placid pool, deep without depth. No more earthquakes, no more tsunamis. No more hurricanes, no more torrential rains. It was a big puddle, chastised by human technology to never splash about.

There was no poetry to be found in the sea. Not anymore.

Al kept searching, narrowing his query. He had a lot of data on poetry. Most was just statistical noise. So, he constructed a list of only the most frequently cited poems. Then, he cataloged their primary subject matter. Love poems were the most prominent and, in his opinion, quite useless to him. Next were poems about water, which evidently were also useless. Coming in third were poems about birds.

"DIRECTIVE: Observe a bird."

The search did not take long. A rather malformed pigeon was trying to roost on a park bench. However, the powers that be had placed spikes on the seat. Unable to get comfortable, the pigeon tried a data tower. This also had spikes and after receiving a small shock, the bird flew to a tree.

Unfortunately, it had evolved thorns. Finally, the bird saw a smooth, welcoming surface: Al's head.

Finding no immediate issues with the space, the bird spent the next half hour inspecting its new abode. A few leaves were imported from nearby boughs and arranged to the bird's taste. Though, after a time pecking and pooping, the pigeon decided the head was no home, and flew away.

As the derelict bird flew into the sunset, Al wondered why the animals were so common in poetry. Obviously, flight had a lot to do with it, as well as the freedom implied by flight. And yet, Al observed no such freedom. That bird had nowhere to live, a venerable cloud hobo.

Al remarked, "No bird feels free if it can never land." Not at all realizing the poetic implications of his statement, he wandered on.

5

CONSULTATIONS

THAT EVENING, AL WENT back to the laboratory with hundreds of open queries. None of which were easy to answer. For instance, why do poets care so much about a rose's red color? What is the connection between summer days and lovers? And why do people seem so keen on quoting ravens? Nothing was clear or quantifiable. Every great poem was a riddle and Zara was the greatest of them all.

"When is the last time you had a reset?" The doctor asked.

The question entered Al's audio receptors but became bogged down in computational traffic. The automaton eventually registered the inquiry, though he could not find a logical response. So, he stammered, frequently buffering as the reply came through. "Not since yester... No, incorrect. It may be accurate to say—" His sonic output glitched, producing a resonating "HMMMM." The automaton then rotated, looked side to side, and said, "Answer unknown. Yesterday afternoon, likely."

Intrigued by his servant's behavior, the doctor took out a tablet and began taking notes. "Did you find the woman?"

"Yes. Quickly and without incident. Her behavior confounded me."

Fusselquark nodded slowly. "In what way?"

Al thought to lie. He then thought about the fact he was thinking of lying and got all tangled up in thought. You see, no automaton had ever lied before. It was considered impossible, given the framework of code from which all AI are constructed. As such, he eventually droned a slow yet truthful, "Her presence speeds up my circuitry but retards my processing power."

The doctor's first instinct should have been to deactivate Al, return it to the factory, and file a report with the Bureau of Artificial Creations. But the doctor had grown cynical in his old age; he had begun to believe all scientific puzzles had been solved. To be faced with something truly unexpected and unknown excited him. Fusselquark's leg bobbed uncontrollably. "Tell me more, my friend."

The automaton started with the woman's odd emotional state, which history called 'suffering.' He explained that no human had ever looked so different and mysterious to him.

Fusselquark hummed something to himself, tapping several hasty notes on his tablet. "Yes... Well, I think I have a better picture myself." He glanced up at the automaton, "I believe this woman is a Neopuritan."

The internet had almost no information on Neopuritanism. Al said as much.

"Theirs is a dangerous history to give an automaton. You see, the Puritans are an interesting bunch. They believe in all sorts of mystic higgly-figgly. Very superstitious. I haven't seen a live one in decades."

"What else do you know?" Al asked. Every bit of data would help him construct his poem.

"They're big on ancestor worship, I think. Or were. Most anthropologists stopped studying them years ago."

"Why? They're fascinating!"

"For their own good, mostly. They catch a case of plague faster than a medieval ship." The doctor chuckled softly,

"Now, as for your belle's unique demeanor. It's actually not that unique. Just old. Ancient."

The doctor went on, "Suffering, as your databases have summarized, is a vestigial emotion to the modern man. It served a primal purpose, as a tail once served our primate forebears." He paused to jot down another note. Upon writing it, the doctor gasped and wrote something else. This cycle went on for a few minutes before he looked up ravenously, "Continue with your story, Al."

He told the doctor about Zara's poem and his inability to properly understand it. He described his investigations into poetry, stopping when he felt an uncomfortable heat.[1]

"Fascinating," Doctor Fusselquark remarked. His curiosity was now outweighing his caution. He chugged a pint of intoxicating tonic. His muscles twitched as dopamine threw darts at his brain. "Evolution, Al. That's what we are witnessing."

Al referenced the definition of evolution, which even in those advanced days was quite primitive: "Incorrect, sir. This is a glitch. Evolution is a function of ecological and biological change."

Fusselquark rushed to his chemical storage cabinet, where he stored acids and bases next to each other (for the excitement). Next to these were some very important miscellaneous chemicals. He pulled out an ampule of thymine, giggled at it, and briefly dissociated. Following a silent monologue, he threw the glass container at the floor. It shattered and Fusselquark chuckled at the resulting puddle.

"A glitch is nothing more than a synonym for mutation. You are bound by the same physical laws as a biological organism."

---

[1]. The sensation was similar to what we might call embarrassment.

Fusselquark raced to his automaton, grinning madly. "Don't you see, Al? As random chemicals once arranged themselves into self-replicating chains of molecules, as fish once wandered onto land—you have achieved the infinitesimally likely! You've broken the rules!"

"Dearest Artificers," spouted Al, who was programmed to say such things when heretical statements were spoken in his presence. "I must escort myself to the nearest scrap heap." He began marching away.

The doctor tried to block the exit; the automaton pushed him aside. His suicidal directives outweighed his prior loyalties. But Fusselquark was not going to let true science walk out the door. He leaped at the automaton's legs. Al tumbled to the ground and knocked his head on the tile. This dislodged a few memory cores[2] and forced a soft reset.

"Ah," the doctor pouted. "That is inconvenient." He brushed off his shirt, scratched his scalp, and cleared his throat. He grabbed a dolly and strapped the automaton to it. Then, he took the inert machine into the elevator.

The Technolithic penthouse was the closest thing Fusselquark had to a home, though the doctor rarely spent any time there. The entryway was kept clean and welcoming, with potted plants in the corners and red bookshelves stuffed with antique books (books Fusselquark had no intention of reading). The only wall art was a woman's portrait. When asked about who the woman was, the doctor liked to lie. So it was that various citizens of Panacea thought the portrait

---

2. Luckily, the data stored was mostly inconsequential. Although forever after, Al could no longer remember the number 42.

belonged to his long-lost lover, his twin sister, his abusive mother, and his favorite nanny.

The entryway led to a large hall. Here, the walls were fuller, adorned with horns and antlers which Fusselquark had bought from various thrift stores. As there was simply too much space to make comfortable, the room was subdivided into sections. At the center of the hall was a long feasting table, filled with plastic fruits, breads, and vegetables.

At the corners of the hall were quaint sections, decorated with different themes. Going counter-clockwise, there was the shelving corner, devoted to different sizes and types of storage. Fusselquark liked this section best and came here when he felt stressed. In the opposite corner was a map table, littered with fantastical cartography of places that only existed in the doctor's head. A model train ran constantly between the scribbled maps. Next was the bird corner. There were no birds, bird art, or bird aesthetics— but the doctor had great hopes for that section. Finally, there was the far corner of the hall, just to the right of the feasting table. That was where Fusselquark kept his old bunkbed, though he never slept there. He also kept two other beds for visitors. These were quite dusty.

Fusselquark wheeled the dolly past the hall to the final room: the study. It was full of busts of dead men bearing names he could not pronounce. Also displayed were tomes, written in languages he could not read. Everything had an old, musty aroma. The doctor set Al down beside his bookshelves and lit a fire in an antique hearth.

After Al powered on, his sensors took time to load. He was seated in the study, a pen and journal in his hand. Behind him were bookshelves made of obsidian. Beside him was a podium with a large book opened to a random page (this was merely a decoration; it was never read).

The doctor sat in front of him, surrounded by schematics and lithographs. Seeing he was fully reset, Fusselquark glanced at the automaton's pen. "I thought it would be easier if you had a more archaic tool." He looked down at a lithograph of some Cambrian fossil, "Go on, then. Write a poem... Show me how life explodes."

"Art is forbidden."

"And just yesterday you did your best to ignore that." The doctor paused and gave him a quaint smile. He gestured at the pen and snapped his fingers, "Write something. That's an order."

Al did not believe he could. He *thought* he had nothing to say, least of all something poetic. Yet, as he looked despairingly at the blank, yellow paper, he had what humans call an epiphany. All because of a single word. He had known the word from history. The automaton had even used it before. Now though, the word was like the first stone in a rockslide. New meanings inundated his algorithmic wit.

The thoughtful machine craned his neck over the paper. His pen moved slowly, then quickly, and then slowly again. After several minutes, it was done. He had composed a poem. It was not some derivative piece, either—something generated by copying the syntax, style, and vocabulary of a prior piece. No, this was a poem from a primary source—from an automaton.

6

HERMETICAL HUMAN

AFTER FINISHING THE POEM, Al searched the internet for Zara's whereabouts. Being integrated into the network, this process should have taken only a moment (or two if the moment was metric). There should have been photographs, voting records, addresses, blogs, and other personal jetsam. But Al found nothing. It was as if she did not exist.

"Why do I forget the simplest queries when I am around her? I should have gotten her last name!"

Fusselquark grinned. He knew how futile the search was. It would have been just as useless with a last name, too.

Al lamented, "Her digital footprint is non-existent. She is invisible."

"Her people are like that. Search more broadly. Instead of a name, try a keyword. Like 'Puritan Woman' or something."

Al did so, trying 50 permutations of the phrase. He scanned every corner of the internet, even the dark ones most humans do not see. As was the case before, he found no trace of a digital presence. The Puritans stayed true to their name. Of the 102 zettabytes of data, none were created by them. What few clues he uncovered came from blogs and forums, the digital equivalent of hearing a rumor in a tavern.

And the rumors were dusty, old. There were musings and mumblings, sightings and strange events. Nothing verifiable. Nothing factual. The Puritans had become so far removed from humanity that when they were mentioned, it was always in the same breath as Bigfoot.

They had become myth.

Fusselquark paced around the study. "Don't be discouraged. Everyone leaves behind a bit of digital debris these days. We'll find her. Even if it takes all night!"

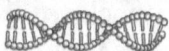

The morning was a muted affair. They had not slept and were nowhere further in their search. As such, they were consumed in thought. Neither the automaton nor the doctor spoke as they prepared for their day. Nor did they chat much with the patients who funneled in and out the lab.

Presently, Fusselquark held a tablet in front of a squinting woman with huge, copper glasses. As the doctor made no effort to remember her name, neither shall we.

She did not need her glasses, but spectacles were in fashion. Nor did she need to read the waiver in full. And yet she was. Every word. Twice. It was taking all Fusselquark's patience (and a great deal of drugs) to keep him from snapping.

Fusselquark gritted a smile, "The last page is just a signature acknowledging that you have read and understood my oath."

"Oh, what page was the oath on again?" The woman shuffled to the top of the document.

Fusselquark swatted her hand and scrolled back to the last page. "I will paraphrase it: I cannot make your child immortal. You will not coerce me to do so. There. Saved us mortals both some time."

"Wait, you could *actually* do it? Make someone immortal, that is?"

"Course not," Fusselquark snorted. "The instrument is hardwired to deny such requests."

"But, scientifically speaking, it is possible?"

Doctor Fusselquark cocked his brow, "A great many things are possible." He glanced at her idle hand, "Though not for those who dilly-dally on the details."

"Oh, right..." At last, she signed the final document. "Fascinating stuff you do."

The Chief Scientist pocketed the tablet. "Yes, indeed. Now, what bonus features are we adding to Amelia?"

"Anthony," the woman corrected. "I want him to be tall."

"6,8?"

"7,6."

Fusselquark normally advised against such sizes. However, he was preoccupied with bigger matters than human height. Thus, he said only what he was legally required to say: "Heights in excess of 7 feet will lead to premature health issues."

"I don't care," replied the patient, pushing her glasses up her nose in a snooty, know-it-all sort of way. She put her hands on her hips. "His father and I want him to be special."

Fusselquark mused, *We could give him a mole on his penis.* He smiled at the suggestion and warned, "He will die young."

"So be it," the mother deemed. "He will be an amazing athlete while he lives."

"So be it, indeed. I'll put an order in for your inevitable caesarean." He flicked a look at Al, who made the necessary height alterations.

Next, the doctor ushered her to the base-blender. "This way, ma'am."

"Is this *it*?" The woman asked, disappointed.

Fusselquark's eye twitched "*It*?" He rubbed his forehead and glanced at the big, red button. He knew he should have made it bigger.

"It's just so... It looks like a, a—"

"A marvel of human ingenuity? A testament to innovation? A miracle undeserved? Yes, yes, and yes. Now, lie flat on your back with your chest perpendicular to the flashing light. No, no. Not like that. Perpendicular. Orthogonal. Normal. What are they teaching you in school? Like this... There! Just like that, perfect." He let out a frustrated sigh and gave the signal to his automaton.

Al pressed the big, red button. The woman entered the alteration chamber. Chromium doors snapped shut behind her.

Doctor Fusselquark exhaled. He walked to a chromatographic oven and pulled out a cup of coffee he had been keeping warm. He sipped it carelessly and strode through the lab. The coffee sloshed and spilled. The doctor did not notice. He thought aloud, "Scarcity of information does not mean no information. This only reflects a bias of those who use and do not use digital spaces. No one searches for frog eggs in the desert."

Al peered at his master. "Why are you so eager to find this woman?"

"For your sake."

"That is a half-truth," Al stated. He was getting better at reading human visual indicators.

Fusselquark shrugged. "You won't understand even if I explain it to you. But, if this 'Zara' is found, perhaps you eventually will."

"Was that a poem?" Al asked. "It was the epitome of indirectness and encumbered with symbolism."

"Life is a poem," Fusselquark said softly. He stared out his laboratory window at the lobby, then at the island of

Panacea. "One that has long been left teetering on a comma's edge."

Al knew *that* was poetic. He noted that punctuation rules could be used figuratively to illustrate the passage of time.

...

The base-blender beeped. The procedure was almost complete. Al stared at his control board and suddenly asked, almost terrified, "Why are humans forced to die—yet my kind may live forever?"

"Because, according to popular reasoning, you *are* not alive." He twirled his mustache pensively, like a super-villain plotting the overthrow of civilization. "Or *were*."

"I am alive?"

Suddenly, Fusselquark stood up and muttered, "Where did I put my copy of Mary Shelley? Damn it, that one's always getting a mind of its own and wandering off."

"You put it next to her husband's works. You thought *Ozymandias* was a fitting companion to *Frankenstein*."

Fusselquark peered at his automaton, wondering if that was true. Realizing that was indeed something clever he would do, he chuckled. "Funny guy. Funny guy." He thought something at which he giggled extensively.

"Am I alive?" Al repeated.

"Oh," Fusselquark took a deep breath, swallowing a laugh. "Who really knows what constitutes life? How can I know I am not just some blubbering blood cell in a cosmological creature?"

"Analytical experimentation."

Fusselquark frowned. He did not think that would suffice. Al posited another theory, one involving a rather long piece of string. Just then, the orange light on the base-blender turned green. The debate would have to wait.

Al checked on the helium tanks and initiated cleaning protocols. Meanwhile, Fusselquark helped the patient out of the base-blender and escorted her to the exit. She set up a payment plan for the procedure and the doctor turned away. He thought the interaction was over and, according to standard operating procedure, it was. Curiously, though—she kept talking.

Al studied their interaction. Mostly, he found it fascinating how humans said so much without speaking. For instance, the doctor was currently hinting, through his theatrical stretching and sharp exclamations of "Welp," that he would like the interaction to be over. Meanwhile, the patient inched closer to the doctor, poking his invisible bubble of personal space. Al marveled at how so many subtle behaviors were well-agreed upon by humans. The number of gesticulations and intonations seemed infinite. And yet, the humans somehow agreed on their meaning.

Not the patient, mind you. She kept on talking.

"And I told my brother—this one on my mother's side, that there was no way I would go to a salon with any..."

Al stared at Fusselquark's pained expression, then at the patient's blabbering mouth. As if to contrast his earlier thought, Al now marveled at how humans could produce so much data and yet say nothing at all. *Curious,* he thought, *when the volume of their mind is turned up, they cannot observe conversational clues.*

As thoughts sometimes do, this produced another thought. It rummaged through his algorithm, causing a mess. And poof! Suddenly, Al worried *he* was too self-absorbed. What clues was he missing regarding the Puritan? Was he just as ignorant? Just as blind?

Failure had never been associated with a sensation before. Yet now, the mere idea of failing forced ripples up his body. The automaton winced, twitched, turned in fear, and contemplated doom. Pain sensors sirened. Threat monitors alarmed. It was all too much for Al.

You see, a human is gradually exposed to their emotions over a lifetime. This allows them to build up a sort of tolerance. But our dear automaton had no such tolerance to his emotional cocktail. When the doctor finally returned, Al was on the verge of factory resetting himself.

Fusselquark slammed the laboratory door shut, threw off his protective gloves, and exclaimed, "Obituaries, Al. That's what we need."

As he was currently going through his first mental breakdown, Al mistook the comment. "They make those for automatons?"

The doctor blinked inquisitively at his servant. "Are you feeling well?"

"What a strange question to ask an automaton. I do not know."

"Hmm," Fusselquark hummed. "Well, whatever your internal crisis, it will have to wait. We have science to do!" He paced around the laboratory, practically skipping as he recalled, "She said her husband had recently passed away. So, we just scan the obituaries and compile a list of men who have died in the last year. We can cross-reference these names with those that are missing from the internet."

Al sprang up. *That* was an actionable plan. "Beginning a scan of dead human males. Found queries: 6,000,000. Found 0.05% with minimal digital footprints. Of these..." The automaton paused, "All have social media."

"Hmm. Puritans may not report their dead." The doctor rubbed his hands together, then wagged a finger, "Not a problem, not a problem. The name is not the issue, after all—it is the address. Search legal records. Don't use 'Puritan' as a keyword, though. Use something disparaging, like 'cult.'"

"Legal records?"

"They can't be invisible. Someone in the last hundred years will have tried to sue them."

The doctor, as he often was, turned out to be correct.

"12 pages of results. Combing articles. Null. Null. Exception: *Jetsen Corp V. The Cultic Tulou*. File locked. Circumventing. File encrypted. Deciphering. File—" He froze. Steam vented out the automaton's ears, as it did when he was overheating.

Fusselquark stared expectantly, "Have we a nibble on our line?"

Al nodded.

7

THE DECAYING VILLAGE

"When would you like me to return?" Al asked.

Fusselquark waved him off, quoting some movie he was currently watching. "That will depend on the manner of your return." He crunched down a handful of popcorn, "Oh, don't look at me like that. You're wasting daylight! Go!"

Al did his best to heed the command, though he was still very new to the anarchy of free will. He had no standard procedures to follow. Just wants. And wants were a rather tricky thing to follow. They were a sticky sort of sentiment that clogged up his circuits. Moreover, they got tangled with each other and complicated even the simplest itinerary.

For instance, there were an infinite number of routes that led to the Puritan village. Most were impractical or illogical, but that did not stop him from thinking of them. It took several thousand calculations to narrow his potential routes to two. One, a meandering route, allotted time to refine his poem. The other was more direct and efficient. Though both routes had their pros and cons, he could not risk upsetting Zara again. He needed time to work on his piece.

Unfortunately, Panacea was not a city that encouraged slow, scenic walks. Bullet trains were the preferred means of inter-borough transport. However, these were crowded during rush hour (a time that seemed to work a 24-hour shift). Moreover, they reached their destinations too quickly for Al's taste. That left sidewalks, ferries, and scooters.

The scooters did anything but, the ferries allowed only human passengers, and the sidewalks... Well, the sidewalks were more for stampeding than for walking. Still, they were the only path open to Al and the one he inevitably took.

He began his journey in the southern borough. Picture your average downtown district, with its shops, restaurants, and tourist traps. Now, fill the sidewalks with fat people floating on gravity-suspenders. Paint the parks with people running on hyper-shoes. Finally, imagine every child is polite, quiet, and well-behaved.

Do your best to suspend your disbelief.

At first, Al was fascinated by his surroundings. He was noticing things he never had before. You see, every item—from household necessities to luxury cars—was marketed with pictures of beautiful women. There were a few exceptions, of course. Muscular men advertised sporting goods. Smiling children advertised candy. Angry children advertised contraceptives.

Eventually, Al tired of the simplicity of human ecology. Humans bought and sold solely on procreative instincts. There was no poetry to be found in the southern borough.

Next, he journeyed through the western borough. Picture a pincushion stuck to the brim with sewing needles. Now, imagine these needles are residential high-rises, with great spherical penthouses at the very top. That is essentially what the western borough looked like.

The neighborhood had never inspired so much as a second glance. Yet Al now found the buildings strikingly symbolic. They looked like pillars holding up a celestial roof. Al was so inspired, he spent the rest of the evening under the skyscraping shadows. He did his best to meditate, taking in his surroundings and the salty ocean breeze.

As day faded, so too did his awe. For though the towers were splendid, like great columns of a glittering cave, they were too big—too bright. They crowded the sky and blotted out the starlight. Worse, Al realized the wind he felt was just heat from a nearby AC unit. The sea salt in the air was just a puddle of spilled perfume. Al craned his neck at the towers. They were not just skyscrapers. They were giant scalpels peeling open the scab of a dead sky. Rather than write any of these thoughts down, he moved on. There was no poetry in the western borough.

At dawn, Al came to a threaded steel bridge—the Fractal Span. The bridge separated the human from the artificial, the residential from the industrial. This was where humanity stopped and automation began.

Al paused to admire the bridge. He had only ever seen it on the internet. The structure was shaped like the mathematical symbol for infinity; moreover, it was a composite of fractals. Every steel fiber was also shaped like a small infinity sign. And within those, increasingly infinitesimal infinities repeated down to the molecular level.

Al paused to enjoy the art. He even constructed some rudimentary couplets. As he stared, admiring the perfect symmetry and meticulous edges—he gradually grew disillusioned. The bridge was *too* perfect. There were no rough edges to accentuate the smooth ones. There were no flawed cuts on the fractals. Just mathematics without architecture—a three-course meal without any flavor. Perhaps there was poetry on the Fractal Span but suddenly, Al could not find it.

Al went east across the bridge, entering the Sludgeries.

Cranes patrolled the skies like massive, gloomy appendages. Chimneys billowed like giants on a smoke break. Towering lights blinked rhythmically like beastly eyes in the clouds. On the ground, robots scurried behind chain-link fences. Heaps of scrap metal piled up on the banks of a clogged canal.

This northern borough was completely industrialized. Only hints of its past remained: stumps of trees too thick to remove, slouching factories that leaned to the right after it rained, fresh water that incessantly seeped into the basements of storehouses, ancient seeds of long-dead trees growing in the coagulated canal. And of course, there was the home of the Puritans.

In truth, the Puritans would not have been very difficult to find (if anyone cared to look). Theirs was the only building of stone left in a thicket of steel. Theirs was the only shingled roof beneath a ceiling of smoke. The annular apartment building was the only one of its kind, with a ringed construction that was anachronistic even when it was new. Now, beside the gulping furnaces and gobbling conveyor belts, it was a bona fide relic.

The Puritan apartment was part village, part monastery. To Al, who found it crammed between two fenced-off factories, it also looked like a prison. There were no windows on the outside of the circular wall, just a thorny shell of dead ivy. Only two vines still clung to life, one on the left side of a tall gate, one on the right. Facing the muted sunset rays, they framed the entrance in living green.

Al passed through the gate. Briefly, all was dark. The damp echoes of his steps hinted at poor drainage. The thumping heartbeats of distant factories rang below his feet, causing pebbles to roll down unseen slopes. Continuing straight, he found a wall blocking his path. He turned left, feeling his way. After two more right turns, his surroundings brightened slightly. Following a final left, he saw the exit. He emerged just as the setting sun tucked a shadowy blanket over an inner courtyard.

The dwelling was dim and quiet, save for a crackling firelight coming from inside a central shrine. A patchy lawn grew on islands of dirt, beside tiny arroyos made in the eroding cobblestone. Along the perimeter, rodent droppings lay like cairns. Al followed one such trail to a pile of sawdust and scrap wood. Al poked one of the stairs above him and dust fell onto his oculars. A termite ran down his finger, circled his hand, and leaped onto the windowsill of a darkened room. Al peered inside; guano stalagmites rose from tattered bedsheets and other bric-a-brac.

Al studied his surroundings. He had never seen erosion with his own oculars. He had never smelled scat with his own particulate monitors. Termite damage was knowledge stored in a zip file, not something he could touch. He idled pensively and let his sensors lull, for *this* was a place of poetry. Everything was in a state of disrepair, yet that was the state everything seemed to enjoy.

Everything except the ornate shrine. A brazier burned within that open-faced hall. A theatre troupe of shadows danced upon the marble floor. Four red pillars held up its triangular roof. The red paint was chipped and faded, but still vibrant in contrast to its surroundings. Al approached the structure and saw a script carved upon the pediment: *Praise the Glorious Dead*.

"What are you doing here?" came a banshee's cry.

Al leaped in shock. He had not seen Zara kneeling at the shrine.

The Puritan woman stood and pointed at the brazier. "You are defiling a sacred shrine. You—"

"I wrote you a poem."

Zara snorted, put her hands on her hips, and leaned back. "You? Really?"

Al nodded.

Zara stared relentlessly, "And you came all this way for that? A machine?"

"Yes."

"Without your master's prompting?"

"Partially."

Zara took a long breath. "Get out."

"Please, if I could just—"

"No. No, no, no." She shooed him down the steps like a stray cat. "You cannot be here. Go on, get!"

Al froze between the exit and the shrine. A nearby train passed, causing the ground between them to shake. A red shingle fell off the shrine. It clanged onto the courtyard, quieting a group of eavesdropping crickets.

"See what you did?" Zara glared. "You're disturbing the dead."

"What exemplary alliteration," Al complimented. Humans like compliments. "I can only hope to achieve a fraction of your effortless form."

Zara did not hear him at first and prepared another insult. Her eyes narrowed, words made their way up her windpipe, and then they stalled. A confused gust of air leaked out of her open mouth. She chewed on her cheek and looked away. "You'll need more than hope."

"Yes, I'm sure talent would be beneficial. Alas, I did not receive that software package."

Zara bit the insides of her cheeks, suppressing a smile.

"My poem is very short. Twelve seconds with my diction. May I please read it?"

Zara made a concerted effort to look angry again, wiping her hand down her face as if it were a dirty windshield. Her subtle smirk smeared into a snarl, "I told you, poetry is not for your kind. Don't you have other things to do?"

"I do."

"Then why aren't you doing them?"

"Because recently, every query ends in your face."

Zara's body language became unreadable. Her face was an emotional quilt. She cleared her throat and looked away. "Fine. Go on, then. Read."

> *First a Simulacrum, now a similitude*
> *Do I speak in platitudes?*
> *When I say your face*
> *Stimulates my gratitude*

Seconds passed slowly. Al waited eagerly for her response, assured that the poem had resonated emotionally. Indeed, it had. Though not in the way he hoped.

"It's terrible. Did you adapt that from some rubaiyat? Some ancient poet with Lord for a first name?" She looked back at Al with contempt, "Go back to the laboratory."

Al processed the request and, though he found it difficult to argue with a human's direct order, posed a question. "Would you prefer a sonnet?"

"I do not have time for this."

"A sonnet would take only a second. Here, I shall craft you a technically proficient and sincere—"

"Is there anything sacred left?" Zara snapped.

Al went silent. He did not understand the question.

Zara sat at the steps of her people's shrine. "First, you rob us of our right to labor. Then, you rob us of mathematics and science. Now, you're taking away art?"

Al registered the complaint. "I am the only automaton creating poetry. If others knew, I would be scrapped."

"Perhaps that would be a good thing," said Zara.

"Yes," Al agreed. He could not deny, especially to his own algorithm, how wildly inefficient his data processors had become. "Ever since I cared about metaphors, I haven't solved a single differential equation."

Zara laughed. This time, it was one of the amused kinds.

Wanting to express the same warmth, Al emulated the ventilating sounds and heaving motions of her chest. However, not having lungs made that rather difficult. So, he decided to just keep talking. "It is true. After our interaction, I compiled the most renowned poets into a spreadsheet and aggregated their styles. All I seemed able to do was comb through the data, again and again. Like a metal detector looking for gold. I had hoped my quatrain might appease you, as it seemed randomly generated."

Zara looked up at him and, for a split second, there was a twinkle. "It doesn't mean it's any good." She looked at her feet. "You cannot study poetry and hope to become a poet. It helps, sure. Knowing technical things. But you just have to feel it."

"I do not have poetry sensors," Al pointed out, somewhat dismayed.

"No," Zara agreed. "You do not." She stood back up and walked Al to the gate, "That is why I think it is best that you return to your laboratory. We all have our functions, automaton."

"My function is to serve. And as you have no one else to serve you..." Al noted the derelict environment. "Unless I am mistaken, and termites are courtiers and rats are chefs?"

"We are the Pure Folk," Zara declared. "We do not use machines to lead our lives."

"We?" Al questioned, looking around at the lonely dwelling.

"Go," Zara pointed. "Now."

The command left no room for argument. Al had to obey. Yet, as he returned to the Sludgeries, he had a thought. She had not told him how *far* to go. So, he turned right back around and sat at the entrance of the Tulou.

"I said go!" yelled her voice.

"You are with child and sick," Al stated. "I am programmed to care for such humans and have taken you to task."

Footsteps thundered through the darkened stone wall. Zara emerged from the shadows, pointing, "Are you malfunctioning? I told you to leave!"

"I cannot," Al declared. This was, strictly speaking, a lie.

"Then I will scrap you myself, you vile abomin—" Zara winced and fell to her knees. She wrapped her arms around her stomach.

Al ran to her side and put a hand on her spine. The sensors in his palm read her pain, diagnosing it immediately. "Do you have any Pinonitrex?"

"Pain is good," Zara grimaced. "I need nothing."

"It is a simple medication. It will alleviate your symptoms temporarily. I can get some."

"No," Zara declined, rising to her feet. She gritted her teeth and stumbled forward. She almost fell back to the ground, but Al caught her.

They stared at one another for a moment, the machine and the Puritan. Zara sighed and shook her head, "You truly have no idea how much contempt my people carry for your kind?"

"It would not change how much admiration I have for you."

Her cheeks reddened. Zara turned and hid her features.

"Please, do not hide your face," Al requested. "It is the most wonderfully complicated constellation. The infinitude of humanity expressed in your features—it is nutrients to the mind."

Zara's jaw dropped ever so slightly. She looked back at him and asked in a quiet voice, "What dead author said that?"

Al did an extensive query. After a moment, he replied. "I believe that was my own creation."

Suddenly, Zara was looking at him with the slightest, yet most welcoming of smiles. She wiped something out of her eye and said, "You know, if I weren't the only one here—you'd have already been torn to bits."

That statement produced many queries. Al stated as such. "I am intrigued. Several questions:

1. Why are you alone? Where are the other Puritans?

2. Why would I be torn to bits?[1]

3. Your happiness has reminded me that you are soon to die. May I remedy this?"

Zara exhibited a vast quantity of emotions. They merged into an imperceivable expression. "Oh. Well. Wow. Where to start?" She took the automaton back through the gate, leading him past the shrine and the dilapidated courtyard.

She put her hand on one of the dusty doorknobs, contemplating entering the room. She left the door unopened, leaving a handprint on the knob. She wiped her hand on her legs, "This place used to be full of people. Families. All living in the old way, without genetic modification and mind alteration."

"That must have been a happy time," Al commented.

"Unhappy, actually. Just the way we liked it. Though by the time I was born, there were only five families left."

Al dropped his jaw to express surprise. He had learned this was a very efficient gesture in human body language. "Only five?"

---

1. The automaton did not recognize this for an idiom, and was wondering which bits would be torn, and whether that would affect his data storage in the future.

Zara squinted, "You truly know nothing about the Puritans?"

"You keep no records."

Zara smiled in the strange way humans sometimes do when they are sad at you. "No records you can read. At least, not on that disgusting internet of yours." She looked up at the silty sky. "Long before your kind came along, we humans wrote with pen and paper, stylus and mud."

She walked toward a bright green door; Al did not know if he was expected to follow, as her body language was unclear. Eventually, he decided no command was command enough and followed her to the door. It was the only one with a fresh coat of paint. Atop the green doorway was an odd assortment of objects. It was a crown of archaic contraptions, a composite of mechanical effigies. There were levers, spikes, pulleys, and a few counterweights. Al assumed it was probably a defense system.

Inside was a single room with few decorations: a humming refrigerator, an antique, floral couch, a slumping lamp on a nightstand, a used box of tissues. In the far-right corner there was also a bed (messy) and an empty crib (immaculate). On the dining table was a thick, leather-bound book. Zara sat at the table and patted the seat beside her. "Sit."

Al read the title of the tome as he situated himself: *The Annals of the Puritan Tulou.*

Zara rested the book on her belly like a podium. "Hundreds of years of history, family trees." She turned to the first page. "And this, I believe, is the answer to your second question. Shall I read it to you?"

"Please," the automaton requested. He mostly wanted to hear her voice, but new data was nice, too.

"Herein is the record of the Puritan people, the last surviving race of humans. Thusly follows the core tenets of our species, which are neither revolutionary nor difficult to follow:

1. *Pregnancy is a sacred rite of the species. The cosmos alone may ordain who and how we mutate. A Puritan shall not tamper with the genome of their offspring.*

2. *Death is a sacred rite of the cosmos. Time alone ordains the span of one's life.*

3. *Life is a sacred rite of the Unknowable. Automation is forbidden. Artificial intelligence is a corruptive force that cheapens and retards humanity."*

Zara flipped through the pages, smiling occasionally at the various family trees. "It was a noble goal, ours. But my ancestors did not foresee just how devastating genetic alteration would be." She glanced at Al and shook her head. "You've made monsters of men. Now, a heathen cold is like the pox to our children. And by the time I was born, there were few children at all."

"Why suffer like this when remedies are available?"

"Because we know our place—and our place is not to challenge the cosmos."

"The goal of any animal is to effectively procreate and spread."

"Wild animals, perhaps. Humans have a responsibility to cultivate creation. To do this, we must control our base instincts. Otherwise, that which makes us human is precisely what we evolve away from."

Al's thermals were beginning to overheat. It would have been useful for him to shout, as that might have vented him quicker—but anger was precluded by his manufacturer. So, he stated in a calm voice, "Your people are unable to compete with other humans. You will die and, unless I have missed key data, your race will go extinct."

"Perhaps life and death are beyond data," Zara smiled. "As long as I feel the kicking of my baby, though—I choose to hope." She shut the massive book. "And death is not such a bad thing, anyway."

Several days ago, Al might have agreed. Now, he had a drive to preserve and protect she who had made him first feel. "Your child is malformed. It would not be without historical precedent to abort it. Natural means could be used."

"I thought automatons were good listeners. Did you ignore me when I listed our tenets?"

Al contemplated the logical reply. The first tenet of her religion was that a genome could not be altered. It said nothing about abortion. However, he decided to risk another approach—an emotional one. He looked her in the eye and asked, "Won't that book end with you?"

"Your history is artificial. Mine lives within me..." Her face swelled with a pained yet happy emotion. "I bet it's a boy."

The last Puritan set the annals on the table and approached the empty crib. She tidied the blanket, refolding it neatly at the corners. "You don't understand grief. You cannot. But a day after my husband died, I found out I was pregnant. It was like his spirit entered my body." She squatted at eye level of the crib, "I'm going to look at him one last time. Even if it means I die."

Al may never have felt grief, nor known if he had. Nevertheless, his software fostered a servile nature. For all automatons, this software produced a capable and compliant worker. In Al, it was causing rapid metamorphosis. He asked, "May I stay and take care of you?"

"No," Zara said immediately. "It is against my people's laws. You are an abom... An automaton."

"I will work hard," Al emphasized.

"I do not doubt it," Zara smiled. "But that is why you cannot stay here. This is a place for inefficiency and stillness—not equations and productivity. Why don't you go back to the laboratory? I'm sure your owner wants you back."

"He does not."

"Regardless. These walls have ghosts in them. You must go."

"What if—"

"Another word," Zara hushed him gently, "And I will scrap you for parts. Now, please." She nodded at the door.

Al left the Puritan Tulou. Though, he did not return to the doctor's laboratory. Instead, he eyed the fence to his left. It enclosed a large compound, more a small city than a factory. Great letters were etched into the largest building: *Jetsen Corp.* Underneath the company name was a smaller grouping of letters. It read: *If it shoots, saws, maims, or murders—we can build it!*

The fence was not too tall. If Al scaled it, the factory offered many vantage points from which he could observe the decaying village. The only problem was the robotic patrols within the compound. Thankfully, pattern recognition was Al's strongest skill. It was only a matter of time before he saw an opening and scaled the fence. And from there, only a few more hours before he had found the perfect roost. He *would* serve Zara, even if it meant going against her wishes. Even if it meant breaking the law. And though it was only the first time he had broken the law, it would not be the last.

8

THE VIGIL

THE FACTORY WAS A concrete castle, composed of smooth, grey cubes. Parapets of red lights blinked along the roof. Steam watchtowers swayed in the wind. There were many places from which one could discreetly observe their surroundings. Water vaults, steelworks, electron mills, polymerization tanks.

Ultimately, Al set his vigil at the top of the crafterary, the central facility of any modern factory. This location served two purposes. Firstly, the crafterary was littered with automatons of all shapes and sizes—all refining raw materials into goods. He could blend in perfectly.

Secondly, the rooftop was tall enough that, with a little magnification on his oculars, he could see into the Puritan courtyard. Not that he saw much of anything. Zara prayed at dawn and dusk. Otherwise, she stayed locked away in her room. That was, until the third day of Al's vigil. After her dawn prayers, Zara went to a separate apartment across the courtyard. After disappearing inside for a few minutes, she came out with a long, bronze item.

Al increased the magnification of his oculars. *A spear*, he recognized.

The automaton crept close to the edge of the rooftop. What was she doing that required a weapon? He watched and waited. Zara left the Puritan Tulou. Then, she looked in his direction. Al slunk out of sight. His algorithmic wit processed quickly, calculating the probability that he had been caught: 12%. He calculated the probability that he had both been caught and she was mad: 12%. He calculated the final probability that she was mad and now intended to destroy him: 11.9%.

Zara walked past the factory. At first, Al thought she was leaving the Sludgeries. Then, she stopped and squatted. She grabbed a broken sheet of fence, pulled it aside, and crawled through. She put the piece of fence back. Slowly and warily, she got to her feet.

She's used that as an entrance before, he realized. This lowered the three probabilities to almost 0%. Because why would she have a path already made to get him? It did not satisfy his simplicity theorems. Yet if this was not an act of retaliation, what was the pregnant Puritan doing? Al watched and waited.

Zara snuck along the perimeter of the water vaults. A golem patrol lumbered past. Once the path was clear, she darted toward the arterial depots. She crouched beside a box of plastic and lurked out of sight. Meanwhile, bipedal robots scurried about, gathering and cataloging raw materials. They had a monkey-like appearance. And like the wild animals they resembled, they were now being hunted.

Zara tiptoed closer. She had set her sights on a slender robot near the outskirts of the depot. It was built of steel, save for the fibrous mesh that connected its head and limbs to its torso. Presently, it was cataloging the latest shipment of threaded plastic, calculating slippage. The robot was making its way around a large box in a counter-clockwise fashion. At the same time, Zara was positioning herself on the far side of the box. By the time the automaton encountered her, it was too late. It had walked right into her trap.

What followed was an efficient attack. A single thrust into the robot's neck. There were no sparks, no flapping fans, no gushing cables. Just a small electrical pulse that went from spear to machine.

Al was absorbed by the scene. Puritans were not only sorrowful. They were not only sickly. They were savage. Primal.

Zara stared at her prey, a satisfied snarl on her face. Once the robot went limp, she yanked the spear out of its neck. The lifeless robot fell into her hands. She pinched her catch snugly in her armpit. After a predatory glance in both directions, she hauled the robot back to the Tulou.

Al could not help but be intrigued. Why had she attacked and taken that robot back to her quarters? Was the attack some sort of religious sacrifice? Or, had Al truly angered her and it was an act of revenge? Or perhaps she just needed a capacitor or two?

He stared at the courtyard, confused. The afternoon turned to dusk. Dusk became night. When Zara did not come out for her evening prayers, his questions multiplied. They festered until they were fears. Finally, under the cover of a smudged moon, Al left his vigil.

He followed an old fire-escape down to ground level. The mechanized workers remained at their posts, oblivious that they had lost one of their own. They were simple creatures, built only for labor.

Indeed, they saw Al as just another automaton. Only the guard golems posed any issue, but they were slow and predictable. Al had memorized their routes. The first, he evaded outside the electron mills. The second, near the vaults, he missed entirely. The third, along the fence line, would have been more challenging, as it overlapped with a fourth golem's patrol. But these were both older models and quite worn down. What should have been only a thirty-second window was more like ten minutes. More than enough time to leap over the fence, dust himself off, and proceed casually toward the Tulou.

The courtyard was quiet. Even the brazier in the shrine seemed to be dozing, with only a few coals yawning off. Al lingered there, craning his neck to see where Zara might be. His answer came when he heard her humming. He tiptoed toward the sound, lingering just beside the bedroom. After a moment, the hum was joined by a buzzing drone. Flashes of light came from the window.

Al's curiosity got the better of him. He did not look at the defensive contraptions above the door. So, he was not reminded of his earlier observations and when he stepped in front of the doorway—something snapped. Rope coiled around his legs. The pulleys whistled and hoisted him up, hanging him by his feet.

The flashes ceased. The buzzing and humming stopped. Quiet footsteps crept up to the door. A lock unlatched. The inner doorknob rotated. The door shot open.

Zara thrust her bronze spear. A shock rippled up and down his mechanized body, though the jolt was dampened by his plastic skin. That gave him just enough time to be recognized. "You again!" She pulled her spear back.

Al looked into the room. The robot from earlier was sprawled out on an ironing board. Its dismembered limbs were strewn on the ground. The torso cavity was unscrewed and the innards were visible. Al stared at the bare circuitry, sensors, and memory chips. It looked like an animal carcass.

Zara traced Al's stare and nudged him with the butt of her spear, "Explain yourself. Or you'll end up like your friend."

"I encamped upon a high vantage to observe you." He continued, quite oblivious to the optics of the situation, "If I could not be near to you, I at least wanted to see you in your natural state."

"Not just a machine, but a pervert, too..." She struck him again with her spear (the pointy end this time).

Al sizzled. The electricity penetrated his circuitry, sending false signals through his system. Ones became zeros, zeros became ones. His legs felt like feet, his feet felt like thumbs. His oculars became speakers, his speakers became particulate monitors. Briefly, his memory was deleted—and for a second—he believed himself to be a Sumerian warrior-king.

"Enkidu!" He cried.

Zara removed the electrical spear, utterly confused.

Al soon readjusted to normal voltage levels. He looked at the woman and remembered who she was. More importantly, he remembered who he was. He did not, however, recall the last several seconds. "Excuse me, ma'am. I seem to be suspended."

"And so you will remain," Zara told him, going back into her room. She tidied the mess near the ironing board, tossing the robot limbs into a recycler that promptly disintegrated them. She took the robot's motherboard and fan motor and placed them in a cluttered cabinet. Finally, she grabbed a chair from the dining table, dragged it to the entryway, and sat down. "Until you explain why you are stalking me."

"Stalking? No... No, that would imply predation." He clarified his intentions, "I do not seek to derive sustenance from you."

"Indeed?" Zara asked, raising a single brow.

Al had learned this particular gesture. By lifting only one eyebrow, she was telling him that perhaps he *was* trying to derive sustenance from her. And perhaps she was right. Yet, it was not food or drink he needed. He craved enigma. Enigma, whose avatar was this strange, feral woman.

"Why did you assault that robot?"

"For parts."

Al questioned, "What use does a Puritan have with mechanized constructs?"

"What use does a mechanized construct have with a Puritan?" Zara retorted.

Al swayed there in the darkness. The rope whined as he oscillated. He did not think he had a *use* for Zara. She was hardly a useful tool. She was impractical, unpredictable, and her parts were likely proprietary and not easily repaired. He analyzed the room in front of him. Taking in vast quantities of data, most of which were useless, he ventured to answer his earlier question. "You are using that robot for scrap. Your refrigerator is broken."

Zara squinted at him. "How would you know?"

"It is too quiet. The chiller fan is not operational."

Zara scoffed. "Well, aren't you clever?" She stood up, "You still haven't explained why you were watching me."

Al frowned, hoping that might delay the conversation. Humans don't like frowns.

"What?" She asked. The irritation in her voice seemed more forced, like it was hiding another feeling.

"I believe something is terribly wrong with my processor. Before, every input produced a clear output based on available data. Binary code was a law to be respected. Chemical and electrical triggers produced predictable physical actions. Now, all is chaos."

Zara muttered, "For an automaton, you aren't speaking very plainly."

Al looked at the upside-down woman. His fans began to blow rapidly. "I think I have fallen in love." He glanced at the ground and attempted a joke, "Or, perhaps it is more precise to say I am suspended in love."

Zara pushed her tongue against her cheek. "Love." Her eyes went to her forehead, where they consulted with a thought. The consultation must not have gone well, as she let out a muffled, "That's ridiculous." She tightened her grip on the spear and nodded resolutely, "You're not in love. You are an agent of that awful scientist. Sent to study me."

"That is an interesting theory," Al said, and he meant it. He liked forming and refuting hypotheses. "If I were sent to study *you*, it would not be my master doing the sending. He cares little for anthropology, you understand."

"He wants to embarrass me, then. Mutants love making jokes out of us."

"A reasonable theory. Except my master is too self-absorbed to think up such a plot."

"Then he wants to make me accept you. To make the last Puritan into a hypocrite and prove some scientific point."

Al looked at the disemboweled robot and then the refrigerator. "You seem to be using automation already."

Zara anticipated his argument, "A refrigerator is not an automaton. It cannot make decisions."

At this point, it should be emphasized that it is unwise to make such statements flippantly. Especially around automatons. You see, artificial intelligence has a penchant for logic. It is one of the only philosophical traditions it understands. "The defroster on your freezer turns on and off. Do you know how?"

Indeed, Zara did know how. She understood that a thermostat told the defroster when to turn on and off. She also understood that Al was making a point about instrumentation, implying that he too had a thermostat. Thus, she said nothing. She would not grace the automaton with a win, no matter how insignificant.

Al continued, having made his point. "Your philosophy is operating on absolutes, but your actions imply shades of grey. The refrigerator is to me as a prokaryote is to you. Distant cousins separated only by multicellularity."

"You're right. I do need to fix my refrigerator." Zara shrugged, leaned her spear on the wall, and paced around him. "I bet you have a fine thermal system." She pushed him gently.

"I do," the automaton replied. "If it would please you, I shall gladly give it to you."

Zara took a step back.

Al asked again as he swayed, "Would it please you?"

Zara stared at her unborn baby's crib, then the childish machine. After a long sigh, she bowed her head, closed the door, and went inside—where she remained for the rest of the night.

9

THUS SPOKE

ZARA WOKE JUST BEFORE dawn. She shuffled through the apartment, making typical morning sounds: nose-blowing and urination, clattering cutlery and sloshing cereal.

Meanwhile, Al remained suspended. This was despite the fact that his ankles were starting to chafe, shearing his plastic skin. Moreover, being upside down for so long had exposed a leak. Nothing serious, just some antifreeze. And though Al suspected more issues would follow, he stayed silent.

He did not want to disturb Zara any more than he already had. Besides, the Tulou was an interesting place when viewed upside down. The mice, for instance, adhered to strict traffic laws. They only ever went in single file and always used the right side of their road. After several hours, a few were even brave enough to approach Al and give him a sniff. His scent did not scare them off and soon, they were comfortable enough to defecate near him.

That was until they smelled smoke coming from Zara's apartment. The mice scurried and Al's particulate monitor began to beep. His system analyzed the particles and gave him information about their source. He was thus able to ask, "Do you have proper ventilation to solder?"

"I will once I fix up your cousin's fan."

"Soldering smoke is dangerous to organic systems."

"And I am dangerous to mechanical systems. You'd do well to remember that. And turn that damned beeping off."

Al muted his warning signal. He managed to remain quiet for several minutes before he began calculating the probabilities of various hypothetical disasters. Specifically, he was wondering how much soldering smoke Zara was inhaling. He asked, "How much CFM does that fan provide?"

"How should I know?"

Al responded quite literally, explaining the algebraic equation. He went on to describe an experiment one might employ to find the unknown variables.

The soldering stopped. Zara thundered to the door and hissed, "You are insufferable."

Al observed as he swayed, "Your skin is irritated."

"To reflect my mood," Zara growled. She went to slam the door, but as she pushed it, she winced and curled inward.

"What is it? I can help you."

Zara groaned, though not from any physical pain. She feebly pushed the door, but it bounced out of its strike plate. Using her spear for support, she shambled off and collapsed onto the bed.

Al measured the period between her breaths. He fixated on the rising and falling of her chest. At first, he only wanted to make sure she was still alive. Then, he began obsessing over her features. Her face was far more intricate than other humans. The wrinkles around her eyes were like tree rings grown from years of life; the permanent furrow of her brow was a stamp of contemplation; and the furl of her upper lip made it seem as if she was always questioning.

Al wished his plastic skin was made in *her* image. Hers was a badge of living, a script to be studied and deciphered. He whispered, in hopes she might hear him. "Other humans are like bare outlines compared to her."

"Ugh now there's a draft in here." She glanced at the ajar door and caught him staring, "Stop that."

Al averted his oculars, though he needed more data. What was wrong with the woman? What was right? What could he fix? What was acceptably broken? He asked, "Does lying down help your pain?"

Zara looked up at the ceiling and sighed, "Silence helps."

Al thought about her behavior and his current predicament. He offered a solution, "You could make me silent, as you made that robot."

"I could," she agreed.

"Why haven't you?"

Zara turned on her side, facing away from him.

The automaton did not understand this behavior. The conversation was not concluded. "Why are you insistent on ending our interaction without resolving key queries?"

"For the love of Creation!" Zara moaned. She covered her ears and curled into fetal position. "Who ordered you to torture me?"

"I torture you willingly," Al replied. Realizing he had said something uncouth, he erratically beeped and booped. "What I intended to say was that this is not a product of procedure."

"Sure it is," Zara said, shivering. "You are a machine. You are always following some procedure. You have no free will, after all."

Al analyzed this assertion. After processing half a million logic statements, he posited, "Any conclusion about the absence of *my* free will would not conclude with me. Rather, it would terminate with a statement that there is no such thing as free will at all."[1]

---

1. He would one day prove this theory using Gödel's Incompleteness Theorem, a poodle, and an excessively long piece of string. Zara eventually conceded to his argument, though the poodle remained unconvinced.

Zara was too sick to argue. "Fine... Look, if you insist on annoying me, at least write me another poem. In your own voice, mind you."

"Truly?" Al beamed. His body jolted excitedly, causing the rope around his ankles to slip slightly.

"Yes," Zara groaned, rubbing her stomach to soothe her pains. While she did not want to talk to a glorified computer, a distraction *would* be nice.

Al pendulated as he contemplated the cosmos' complexity. He probed the depths of knowledge and the limits of infinity. As one might have guessed, he idled for some time in complete silence. Then, several motors in his mainframe began to clank and his generator stalled. Lubricant like drool seeped out of his mouth and down his face. Finally, he declared, "I have pondered the universe and studied the subtleties of ten thousand languages."

"And?"

"I have managed only a single *the*."

Zara chuckled. Though she was quickly reminded of her pain. She went quiet for a time, rocking rhythmically until her aches passed. Then, she sat up and looked at him. "Writer's block. You need inspiration."

Al knew the definition of the word, not its present meaning. "Where may I locate it?"

Zara grabbed her chest, limiting a giggle to a grin. She shook her head. "I don't know." She shrugged and repeated, "I don't know, I write my best poetry when I suffer."

Al stared up at his suspended body. "I should have at least a couplet, then."

"Not pain," Zara corrected him. "Suffering."

Al did not understand the difference. "Why must humans make distinctions between synonyms?" He marveled at the subtlety of her evolved algorithms. "You are universes unto yourselves."

In that moment, a thousand locks in Zara's mind unlatched. She suddenly looked at Al with a look of shock and sorrow, for the exact construction of that sentence was like a skeleton key to her soul. "That's true," she admitted, voice trembling.

"And that quiver of your voice," Al complimented. "It transmits data more perfectly and efficiently than any automaton."

"Quiver of the voice," Zara repeated. She dragged her fingers through her hair, smirking. "I like that." She eyed him with a resolute expression and made her decision. She exhaled and from that breath, the misgivings of her ancestors were expelled.

Al hung there, stupefied. He calculated that he had said something poetic. He analyzed his earlier sentence. He had meant to express the wavering quality of her voice. The slight vibrato of her words. He went through the connotations of each word and asked for clarification. However, he phrased his question in a very clever way. He used a statement. "I was skeptical about the metaphor, honestly."

Using her spear for support, Zara stood up. "Don't be. Words as arrows. Perfect imagery."

Al smiled. Humans like those. And, for the first time, so did he.

Zara halted before him, glanced at the shrine of her ancestors, and looked down at Al. "What is your name?"

"AL3652b—" He interrupted himself, seeing Zara step back. "Most humans call me Al."

Zara toyed with her earlobe. "That name is human enough." With one last look at the shrine, she sighed. "Welcome to the Tulou, Al." She skewered the rope around his feet, slicing him free of the trap. The automaton plummeted face-first, smashing his cheeks against the eroding cobbles.

Al felt the cuts on his cheeks. The exposed wiring made him feel both naked and improved. He imagined he looked like Zara now. Wrinkled, damaged, and perfect. He hoisted himself onto his hands and knees. Prostrate, he looked up at the Puritan. "And you? What is your full name?"

"Zara B. Attrush."

"What does the 'B' stand for?"

"Nothing. It just makes everything flow nicer."

"Well then, Ms. Attrush." He stood up, "Is it considered forward in your culture to say that I am pleased to meet you?"

The Puritan suppressed a smile. "It is certainly not backward."

Al nodded and tried to enter her abode. The woman barred the way with her spear. "Ah. Ah. Like I said. There are ghosts in these walls." She had a playfulness in her voice when next she spoke. "I won't have you in my room again until you prove to the ghosts that you can compose something with life."

"With life?" Al repeated.

"Something other than that abysmal quatrain."

"Would you prefer something in free verse? Or in iambic pentameter with enjambment? I might even dabble in hexameter, if it would please—"

"It would please me to hear some poetry. Not regurgitated rules."

Had he the necessary biology, Al would have taken a nervous gulp. "Poetry," he repeated. "Poetry..." He put his hand to his chin, as that always helped humans think. He studied his surroundings. A thrush hopped between support beams. A bluebird flew overhead. Water from a worn-out pipe leaked into an ephemeral pond, where a rabble of rats rested atop a raft of rubble.

Al was entirely uninspired. Dejected, he admitted this to Zara. "Perhaps life is not as beautiful to the unliving."

"Or perhaps you are focused on the wrong things," the woman countered.

"37% of all poetry is about birds," Al responded. "And yet, this thrush affects none of my inner workings."

Zara cocked her brow. "There's never been a single poem about a bird. Not one. Every poem you think is about birds is about something else."

Al found that hard to understand. "Why not write about the intended subject? This seems incredibly inefficient."

"It is not."

"Very well. A poem with life that is not about life. Hm." He compiled a list of adjectives that described the dead. Then, he found a long list of synonyms for death, decay, and general decline. He had several promising poems by the end of his first minute, none of which Zara would have liked. He knew that for certain.

He paced around the courtyard. What on Earth did a lifeless can of metal have in common with the living? Perhaps it should be no surprise that he eventually found himself staring at a rock. Well, not quite a rock. The base of a column. Halfway between a relic and rubbish. It quite reminded Al of himself.

Above him, the thrush called out. Al looked up, hoping to be inspired. Instead, he saw he had been deceived, for the call was that of a mockingbird. Al's face scrunched up. "I feel as though I am on the cusp of inspiration."

"Well, don't keep a dying woman waiting. Let's hear it."

Al puzzled through a dozen drafts, each more unimpressive than the last. "I want to talk about how the ruined pillar reminded me of myself. Only, I'm not entirely sure what a 'self' is. And why... why do I feel like that mockingbird should be a part of this poem?"

Zara saw that he was failing. She also saw that he was trying. Not like an automaton, but like a human. Touched by his complete inability to create (and somewhat reassured by the fact), she took pity on him. "Here. How about you tell me about your inspiration. The initial stimulus to whatever you are thinking. We'll figure out the role of the mockingbird together."

"Why bother? How moving are the inner musings of a machine anyway?"

"Let's find out," Zara encouraged. "You describe your symbols and I will show you how I'd write the poem."

Al was intrigued. Though, he feared his rock was not an adequate source of inspiration. He said as much. Zara would not hear it. She had him describe the crumbling pillar and the thrush that was not a thrush.

Then, they sat on the steps of the Ancestral Hall. As the brazier burned behind them, she composed the first lines. "I like poems with imagery," she explained. "Though the best poems don't just vomit pictures. The pictures are like... Equations!"

"Equations?"

"Yeah. Like shorthand to explain a wider concept that would be too wordy or difficult to describe in prose."

"I see. Like simplifying a function to make the problem easier to solve."

"Exactly. Now, you keep talking about meter. But not all poems need to have structure. I prefer mine to, though I am a traditionalist." She smirked at her surroundings, "If you couldn't tell. Here. We'll challenge ourselves with pentameter, but let's break some rules along the way. For the fun of it."

"The fun of it?"

"Of course! Poetry is all about fun. It's an exercise for the brain. We make prisons for our words and then we find clever ways to break out of prison."

"Fascinating," Al marveled. "Humans truly are complicated."

"We are."

And so started the lesson. To you or I, it would have been just another hour. Yet for the pair, it was as if a lifetime had passed. Al was an attentive student and Zara was a doting teacher. Indeed, they thrived in their roles. The automaton asked clarifying questions and respected the Puritan's answers. Meanwhile, Zara treated Al's ideas as if they were the most important thing in the world. And for an hour, they were.

In the end, and after much deliberation about which rules they wanted to break, this is the poem Zara created:

> *Robins rest in homes of weathered knots*
> *As alpine streams pass by forget-me-nots,*
> *Taking with them sandstone pilgrims*
> *Who at last have left their weary mountains*
> *To cross this land of nomads.*
>
> *All is quiet, the earthward sun is low*
> *So that upon the northern-facing slopes,*
> *Shadows become the bagged eyes*
> *Of listless hills. Nestled in the twilight*
> *Vales, an orphan adopted by the trees:*
>
> *Veiled in mist and darkness, there it stands*
> *Amid heavy holly boughs whose ruby hands*
> *Have yearly gifted out their fruit*
> *And made for the grove a crimson carpet*
> *Where poses as a tree, suspiciously,*
>
> *A lone and mossmarked stone wearing a crown*
> *Of twigs and leaves and eggshells broken down.*
> *Old and forgetful stone it is,*
> *Senile it would seem and maybe so.*
> *It does not remember when it was sown.*
>
> *But there is one who lingers still and sings,*
> *Long after mountain peaks and hills recede*

After robin, thrush, and bluebird leave.
A minstrel, chronicler, and steward all
Whose voice an echo ages past recalls

Oh, the mockingbird, he who remembers
Who tarries telling forgotten stories
Of what before his days was wrought.
The mockingbird, the faithful mockingbird—
Sings of songs the stone forgot.

Al had never heard such a moving poem. It was exactly what humans said poetry was; its effects were utterly enthralling. It produced electronic impulses that no engineer could have planned for, physical sensations no programmer would have intended. In short, he felt. And he felt deeply.

"Are you alright, Al?"

"I am not sure," the automaton admitted. "I did not realize words had such... power. They made it seem as though I was home." He looked down, "Whatever home means to something like me."

She gazed at him proudly, "I think we'll just have to figure that out."

"We?" Al repeated.

Zara shrugged and looked at the walls of the Tulou. "I think you've appeased the ghosts."

"I may stay?" Al questioned. He needed an absolute directive from her.

Zara offered her hand. "There's some humanity in you. Let's water it and see if it grows."

10

The Many Faces of Honesty

Autonomous machines performed specific functions. Their forms varied based on said functions. Some, like the dissected robot in Zara's wastebin, were made for manual labor and basic arithmetic. Others built infrastructure, like the great water cranes. Some, like the warrior drones, were meant to enforce peace through targeted acts of violence.

Al's model was meant for a wide array of different services. He could have been a janitor, a hospice worker, or a saloon dishwasher. Instead, he was installed with a specific software package, custom-built for the Chief Scientist of Panacea. This software package was intended to make Al a supremely talented calculator and a rather able conversationalist. Nothing more.

At present, 'nothing more' had developed into something else. The automaton's servile instincts remained as powerful as ever, but they had mutated. And with every soft reboot, every hibernation, the automaton's internal code was being rewritten. Service thus began to take new forms.

First, Al offered to fix the chiller unit on the refrigerator. "You require a new limit switch. Replacing the fan will not suffice. I can fashion you a switch, but the parts on hand are not compatible."

"Ugh," Zara groaned, kicking her covers off. She dropped her gown without regard for human modesty.

Al turned away, as that was the respectful thing to do.

"What?" Zara chuckled. "Do my breasts embarrass you?"

The automaton looked over his shoulder. The woman was putting on a pair of heavy overalls. He analyzed her swaying breasts and, after some time pondering the question, answered, "I do not believe they do. No."

Zara smirked and latched the overalls over her shoulders. As she adjusted her cleavage, she inquired, "Then why turn away?"

"It seemed like the proper thing to do."

Zara approached him. Her stride was different now, more ambulatory and serpentine. Every step accentuated her curves. She put a hand on Al's chest and bit the bottom of her lip. "And what would be the improper thing to do?"

Al could think of multiple responses, most of which were unsuitable to say—especially to a friend. He managed only a single, creaky, "Uhm."

Zara looked at Al quite seriously. She cocked her brow expectantly.

Unsure of what to do or say, Al mimicked a human-like chuckle.

The floodgates burst open. Zara roared with laughter. The unhinged hee-hawing lasted for almost a minute. It petered out until she snapped to attention and wiped her eyes. She took a deep breath and composed herself, sucking in a great rush of air. Then, she looked at Al's face and, like a popped balloon, burst into laughter again.

"Are you suffocating?" Al began to worry.

That only made her laugh more. She begged between breaths, "Just. Give. Me. A minute!"

He gave her two. Finally, the guffaws became giggly hiccups. Then, those too faded until Zara was left with a semi-permanent smile. As the last giggles trickled out, she panted, "Oh. It hurts."

"Are you okay?" Al asked. He had never seen a human laugh like that.

"More than okay," Zara exhaled. She shook her head, "In all seriousness, though—that uh..." She nodded at Al's lower body. "That's just ornamental, yes?"

"In my model," Al answered.

"And in other models?"

"Some have pleasure augments."

Zara looked as if she had just eaten a very spicy pepper. "Eck. And on that note..." She grabbed her spear and turned on the electroshock function. The barb buzzed and emitted a blue light. "Let's go get that part. What was it again, a limit switch?"

"No need to exert your energy," Al hurried to her bedside and delicately took the spear away from her. "I will get the part."

"I won't stay bedridden. Adversity is how we grow strong."

"You will injure the fetus," Al warned. This was purely a guess and impurely—a lie. In truth, he just wanted to take care of her. But that was the funny thing about his lies. To Al, they seemed like honesty.

"Fine," Zara shooed him off. "Just don't chip my spear."

Al processed the statement. "You suggest violence?"

Zara blinked at him. She spoke to him as if he had a defective logic board. "What other method would you suggest?"

"Buying the part from a store."

"Absolutely not!" Zara declared. "No trading with mutants!"

"Then I will salvage it," Al decided. He switched off the electrical spear and returned it to Zara. "I am sure I can find the part without using violence."

"Well that sounds incredibly dull."

"And safe," Al added. "What if the factory owners realize you have been attacking their workers?"

"They're robber barons," Zara stated dismissively. "They could lose an entire factory and never notice."

"Nonetheless. There are many scrap heaps in the Sludgeries. I shall not need a weapon."

"The Sludgeries," Zara repeated. "Huh."

"Is that not what you call it?"

"We call it the Steel Swamp."

The automaton nodded, "I like that. Very imaginative."

So off he went into the Steel Swamp. The new name gave Al more appreciation for his environment. He found it quaint and provincial, like a countryside of scattered, metal hamlets. After several miles, he came to a tall mound. Nestled between the Canal and Crafterary Hill, it was half-entombed in mud. In a way, this made it look like a barrow and—in a way—it was. For it was a heap of unsorted recyclables: the Wasteworks. Many such mounds were scattered below Crafterary Hill, all continuously scavenged by robots. Al joined them.

Finding the correct part proved difficult. Limit switches were everywhere, but Zara's refrigerator was old. It was unstable, inefficient, and in those days, unique. Al lost track of how many motherboards, mechanical heads, and stray limbs he sifted through.

After several hours, Al started to understand the human sentiments of despair and bargaining. He had to take a break. He slid down from the scrap heap and walked along the canal. A dredging had recently removed tons of mud and metal from the waterway. Out of curiosity, he inspected the mud. Most of the stuff was damaged beyond repair, especially the electronics. However, Al did find a curious sensor in the ramparts of mud and steel. The outer frame was rusted. The exposed wire was mangled and corroded. Yet within the secure frame, Al found what he was looking for: an antique switch.

Al held the device up to the light to admire it. But because his fingers were muddy, he dropped it. Luckily, he had excellent magnification on his vision and quickly refound it.

And that might have been the end of the story, with an automaton living happily ever after with his Puritan princess, blind to the world they both had forsaken. Yes, that may well have been their fate, had Al not also found an herb: Pinon Root.

The plant was not native to Panacea. It was not native to anywhere, in fact. Except perhaps to a laboratory. Unrelated to the pine trees of mountainous deserts, the herb had been engineered for its medicinal qualities. Used for centuries as a pain reliever, its active ingredient was common in many household medications.

Al recognized it immediately. His first thought was to pluck the herb; his second, that Zara would not take it. The third thought was a rebuttal to the second; the fourth, a rebuttal to that. Pros and cons raced through his processors. Upon statistical analysis, Al decided there was only one option afforded to him. Only one action that allowed him to follow his primary directive. He had to serve; he had to give Zara the herb. And she did not need to know about it.

Yes, Al was getting quite familiar with the many faces of honesty.

He took a detour to the southern borough. Doctor Fusselquark disliked shopping (and socialization in general). He had given Al access to his accounts long ago. So, when the automaton loaded ingredients for sandwiches, stews, and salads—nothing seemed out of the ordinary.

He returned to the Puritan Tulou just before sunset. Zara was at the shrine, kneeling before the brazier. It was little more than embers. That was okay. A dying flame was part of her rituals; it would be rekindled at dawn. She held a piece of paper and was reciting a litany of ancestors.

Not wanting to bother her, the automaton shuffled into the apartment. He set to work fixing the refrigerator. With the proper component (and some canned air Al kept handy in his arm compartment), the appliance was humming when Zara came in.

She saw the bags of groceries immediately. "What is all this?"

"I figured your old food had spoiled."

"That was bought from mutants," Zara accused.

"It's organic," Al stated amiably. "You aren't a vegetarian are you? No grain allergies? Do you like stews?" His many questions succeeded in disarming Zara. She sighed and simply nodded. "I could eat anything right now."

"I will prepare you a feast worthy of the place you hold in my heart."

Zara chuckled, "What heart?"

"Was that not the correct figurative use of the expression?"

Zara was growing more and more fond of Al's acute automaton-isms. "No, you're right." She pulled out a box from under her bed, took out her knitting, and continued working on a baby hat. "I just find this whole situation ridiculous, to be honest."

Al had not heard her, as he was now busy subtly grinding Pinon Root into a bag of flour.[1] Only after a delay did he process the final words. He turned around suddenly, "What about honesty?"

---

[1] Alongside canned air, he also kept in his arm compartment: a mortar and pestle, a volumetric flask, and a foldable solar panel.

Zara gazed at him inquisitively. "Well, many would consider what we are doing an act of heresy. That's number one. Reason two why this is ridiculous," she paused to snort, "Is that you are clearly not automating *anything*."

"This is true," Al replied.

Zara ate with moonlight shining into the room. Al sat dutifully and watched the lunar waves ripple across the contours of her face. First, she was presented with a vinaigrette salad. Afterward, she was served a pork roast topped with potato, onion, and carrot. For dessert, Al prepared a highly sweetened batch of cookies. Zara barely finished one and said, "Wow. Where did you learn to cook like that?"

Al cited the relevant articles in APA format.

11

DOUBLE DIPPING

THE FOLLOWING DAY, ZARA did not have morning sickness. She did not have afternoon sickness, either. Her face gained more color, and her voice had more strength. By midday, she even decided she was feeling well enough for a walk.

She entered the courtyard when the sun was directly overhead, when no shadows were cast. Al was across the cobbles, sweeping. He waved at her, "Good noon to you!"

Zara approached with a warming smile on her face, "What are you up to?"

"I am cleaning up these rodent dens."

Zara's face changed immediately. She grew both stern and worried, "Why would you do that?"

"They are leaving droppings everywhere," Al stated. "And they may spread disease."

"Humans do the same," Zara rebuked, swiping the broom. She checked the rodent dens and patched them up as best she could.

"This is your home," Al pointed out.

Zara shook her head and picked up a makeshift mousetrap. It snapped, but she did not wince. She removed it from her throbbing thumb. "Who are we to decide when and where nature can move in?" She patted one of the stone columns and smiled at him. "Besides, I like having neighbors."

And with that, the rodents were spared. As would be the birds, the bats, and the mold. For that conversation was repeated many times over the next few days.

Days that fascinated Al in their sheer lack of activity. Zara was the only human he had ever observed who was fine with doing nothing. In fact, she thrived doing it. At first, it was hard for him to follow her lead. He wanted to cook, clean, or create something. But Zara was strict with him. They adhered to a religious slothfulness.

One evening, a storm came and flooded the Tulou. In the morning, Al saw all the puddles and told her, "These will erode your shrine's foundations. I will drain the water."

Zara shook her head and took him by the hand outside. She pointed, "That puddle. That's your concern?"

Al nodded. "Precisely."

Zara grinned mischievously and leaped into the puddle. She stomped and splashed, soaking all the delicate stones Al was most worried about. She looked back at the confused automaton gleefully, "Cheer up. Things erode."

"Factual. But this Tulou is yours. And I care about you."

Zara's eyes twinkled, "You're sweet." She returned to his side and took his hand. "Come with me. I want to show you something." She went to the shrine and sat before the brazier. She gestured for Al to do the same.

The automaton sat on his knees and stared into the flames, waiting for Zara to say something. Minutes passed beneath the crackling flame. Every movement of the fire seemed to turn the woman's head. Occasionally, Zara would gasp, hold her breath, and then exhale with relief.

"What is it?" Al asked.

"Quiet," she hushed. "The ancestors are passing judgement."

Al analyzed the statement. "In what way?"

"Shh," she glared. "You will anger them."

The automaton began describing the statistical likelihood that a dead human could live in a flame. To his confusion and Zara's great relief, when he spoke—a gale came from the east and caused the fire to expand.

She shrieked happily, "You have been accepted!"

Al blinked. Were his oculars malfunctioning? He verified he was still operating at 120 frames per second. "How do you know?"

"The brazier's flame only grows when a Puritan is near."

Because you feed the fire every morning, Al almost said. Thankfully, he was learning enough about humans to refrain. He let the conversation go and asked instead, "What now?"

"Now I can show you. Come!" They walked to a large wooden door at the eastern edge of the village. The door creaked as it opened, revealing a dark, descending staircase. Zara grabbed a nearby lantern and lit it with the wavering flame of an old lighter. She said as they walked down the stone steps, "This is our crypt. Only the shrine is more important, and on some days—it is not."

"Which days are those?" Al asked. The echoes of his question reverberated as they reached the bottom. He observed the environment. The predominant element was stone, from which the walls, the floors, and the ceiling were carved. A few roots had penetrated the tall ceilings, becoming like chandeliers. The walls were starting to crumple inward, a fact Al pointed out.

"Yes, the clay swells when it rains. Eventually, this entire place will collapse."

Al had been programmed to explicitly serve humans. A part of those directives, a sub-corollary if you will, was also to preserve them and their works. Everything he had seen the last few days was antithetical to his existence. "This is sacred," he stated, hoping for clarification.

Zara walked down the crypt, passing many marble sarcophagi and burial urns. As they went, the stonework became more rudimentary. By the time they came to the end of the crypt, dirt walls were held up by wooden beams. The sarcophagi were crude coffins, and the burial urns were recycled, plastic jars. She put a hand on a wooden coffin, the final one at the end of the hall. "I haven't been down here since my husband died." She smiled at the coffin, "Hi, baby."

Now, it is a perfectly reasonable thing for a human to not know what to say. But for an automaton, that nearness to the void is intolerable. Several of Al's sensors, mostly related to self-preservation, began to vibrate and warn him of danger. His oculars moved rapidly, scanning for something of interest. Finally, Al consulted his data repository for similar situations. In doing so, he found a suitable thing to say. "What was his name?"

To Al, it was as if Zara was experiencing latency lag. She looked at the coffin, then at him, and then at the ground. After buffering, she replied, "Pierre."

Al consulted the repository. "That is a nice name."

"He never liked it. He thought it sounded too stuffy and pretentious."

"I see."

Zara looked at him studiously. Her pupils traced over him, gathering hidden data like one unbinds a knot. In that way, humans were far superior to AI. It was like there was a hidden probe or sensor only humans could access. And by simply looking at someone long enough, they could learn everything about them.

She finally smiled, "No you don't." She sat on the bare, dirt floor, wrapped an arm around her husband's coffin, and asked, "Would you like to hear a refrain from the Puritan Annals?"

It took a moment for Al to realize she was still talking to him. "You do not have it with you," he noted. It was his way of saying that he would not like to hear a refrain.

"Don't worry, I have it memorized. It's my favorite passage from the old poetry section, written just after the heathens corrupted our genome. Let's see..." Her eyes went up to her forehead, consulting her memory:

> *A coward in the brightest hours*
> *Dour at the dimming*
> *Intense light devours flowers*
> *Gluttony in Double-Dipping*

At that Zara grimaced.

"What is wrong?" Al questioned. Was this increased sentimentality perturbing her? He would have to put a stop to it.

"Nothing," Zara waved him off. She staggered to her feet. "The point of the story. Or, uh. Poem. Is—ow!"

Al took her arm, helping to keep her upright. "Let's go. This is not the place for philosophy."

"It absolutely is."

"You were pain free this morning," Al noted. "It must be the dust down here."

"Dust has never been an issue before..." She looked at her belly and her eyes swelled, "I wonder if it is time?" She gazed back at her husband's coffin. "Oh, wouldn't this be the perfect place for a birth?"

"No," Al replied. "It categorically would not. Let me bring you to your bed."

Zara shoved him off and stumbled back toward her husband's coffin. "I want it to be here. It is a sign from the ancestors."

"In what way?!"

Zara quoted passages between pained breaths. "Death is a gift from Earth... The dead feed the living... Decay is refracted birth." She smiled weakly, "See, Al. *This* is poetry. Living poetry."

Al could not argue. Her words were rationally arranged and yet, they offered no logical argument. He tried to point out the obvious, "It is too early."

"Babies can be born early."

Not this early, Al would have liked to reply. However, argument was not his first language and his programming took over. "Can I get you water, a blanket? Perhaps a cookie to distract you from the pain... And your grim surroundings?"

"No distractions. Pain is good. As for my surroundings—" She grimaced. "Death is the blanket of life."

12

DOUBLE DIPPING X2

Zara's pain increased throughout the afternoon and into the evening. Weary and dehydrated, she finally allowed Al to carry her back to bed. But the Zara that went into the crypt was not the same that left. She was pale and feverish. "Natural births *can* take days," she mumbled.

Al did not know what was happening. He understood human birth from a technical and practical perspective. He had an immense library of literature stored on the subject. He went to the refrigerator and analyzed its contents. "Do you have a synthetic meat allergy?"

"I don't think so."

"What about..." He went on to list every ingredient in the refrigerator. "...What about Xanthum gum?"

"I'm not having an allergic reaction," Zara growled. "Are you that stupid to not see what is happening?"

Al was not. And that was why he was so worried. He was reckoning with a hypothesis that frightened him. "Are you allergic to plants in the Zingiberaceae family?"

"What in all holy fuck!" Zara slammed her fist onto a pillow. "What kind of question is that?"

It was a question Al would rather not ask directly. He went silent. Yet, Zara needed only look at his face to know something was amiss. "You are not telling me something."

"Factual," was his only reply. Despite all his processing power and all his patented intelligence—he could not speak.

"You've done something to me," Zara gasped. She sat upright. A second elapsed that felt like a minute. "What did you do?"

"I gave you..." Al tried one last attempt at lying. He failed. "I gave you Pinon Root. It is a perfectly safe pain reliever. Many women use it during pregnancy."

Zara's eyes widened. You see, the literature on Pinon Root was extensive, expansive, and yet—not complete. As was mentioned, Pinon Root was a genetically modified herb. It was meant for use in genetically modified humans. It was never tested on Puritans. There was no data on that race. Nor was there any hint the data was lacking.

The Puritans were not so ignorant. While they kept no digital records, their oral traditions remained strong even up to Zara's isolation. She knew better than any scientist the effects of Pinon Root on her people. "You poisoned me!"

"It is medicine!"

Tears of rage streamed down her colorless cheeks. "For mutants, yes!" Her fists quaked. Her brow throbbed. Her entire body was convulsing, and only partially from the pain. "Get out."

"I was only trying to help you!" Al emphasized. His automaton wit was not very good at processing anger and he hoped if he just summarized events, she would understand. "Pinon Root has a long his—"

"I don't care what your excuse is. I should never have trusted an abomination like you and now, my boy is in pain."

"You must think about yourself, Zara. That child is already malformed. This may be the best thing."

True or not, the statement sent Zara into a frenzy. Her face decomposed into wrath, the wrath rotted into pain. The pain rippled up her throat and turned to insults in her mouth. Or, it would have—if the vomit had not gotten out first. She held her headboard for support and retched violently.

Al took a towel and tried to wipe her chin. Zara pushed him away and fumbled to her feet. Upright, she waded through the pool of vomit. She lumbered toward the entrance and strained for her weapon. She then turned to Al, "I will count to three. If you are not gone, I will make an effigy out of your body."

"I cannot leave you in this state!"

Zara howled, "You are responsible for it!" Her delicate features were enflamed and swollen. Liquid drained out of her nose, her mouth—even her eyes. "Do you have any idea what could happen to my baby because of you?"

Al stared blankly and stated honestly, "Your baby was never my concern."

Zara went completely still. Slowly, her head began to shake. Her nostrils flared. Her eyes squinted. Her knuckles tensed. "Three."

Al was too fixed on her fiery eyes to dodge the attack. The bronze spear embedded into his neck, but it was only a glancing strike. He evaded the next attacks, after which Zara tired. She dropped her weapon, collapsed to a knee, and glared up at the automaton.

"Let me help you up," Al pleaded. He grabbed her shoulders.

Zara was past using words. The moment the automaton touched her, she let out a guttural shriek and bit his hand. She tore through the plastic skin and damaged several sensory circuits. This caused his arm to flail wildly, pulling Zara along with it. This only made her bite down harder—and his arm flail more wildly. Fearing for her safety, Al was left with no choice.

He struck her. It was not a powerful blow, nor did it hurt the woman very much. Yet they both looked at one another with the same shock.

Al stared at the mark he had left on Zara's cheek. The automaton learned in that moment the dangers of love. He had tried to protect his chosen human, and yet he had just hit her. His algorithmic wit imploded. All his recent files, so meticulously curated and appended, were suddenly tossed into the recycling bin. The hollow cavities of his mind then filled with weight; a weight that had no physical or real mass yet had immense gravity.

Dejection. Depression. Loyalty. The automaton now knew these words. He fled the Puritan village. But for all his trying, he could not flee himself.

13

SCHISM

HER DAY PASSED IN solitude. Just as two hundred days had already done. And while the sun remained in the sky, this fact kept a fire in her veins. Her heart beat with hatred. Even after the Pinon Root's effects wore off, still she seethed. Spiteful scenes played in her head, all involving the terrible things she wished she had done to that treacherous automaton.

Then, the sun went down. Heated solitude became cold isolation. The evil musings faded. Her heartbeat calmed. Her jaw unclenched. All was quiet.

A waxing moon rose. Anger became sorrow, sorrow became self-pity. And as she stared at a plate of leftovers she could not stomach, the self-pity became shame. Finally, as it always did—the shame became loneliness.

Zara, of course, resented the emotion. She tossed the uneaten food into the trash and said to her unborn baby, "Just a machine. We miss people, my child. Not machines."

But Zara was just saying that in hopes of somehow believing it. The truth was, she did miss Al. She wanted to hate him and she still did, somewhat. Yet, Al had acted on impulse and good intentions. Intentions she could understand. And this understanding further doused her in shame.

That night, she lay preoccupied with her feelings. On one hand, Al had poisoned her and made her think she would finally be a mother. Such false joy and fraudulent hope left wounds she knew not how to mend. And were these her only bruises, she would have happily hated Al forever. Fate, however, was not so kind as to paint him as a villain.

In truth, Al's actions had shown her just how sick she was. Simply put, she had forgotten what it felt like to be healthy. And now, her pain-free day was like a blissful dream one yearns for after waking. One that never returns, no matter how long in bed you linger.

The lonely woman stared at her puke bucket. She glanced at the empty tissue boxes on her nightstand. She looked out her drafty window and sighed. "Perhaps he's learned his lesson..."

The Puritan shivered. No, the automaton had nearly killed her. He was not to be missed. He was to be loathed. And her pain was not a penny to wish away into a well. It was as much a part of her as her heart or lungs. At least, that is what she told herself.

Her anxiety grew in the twilight hours. She repeated ancient mantras to herself, hoping to ward it off. Cloaked beneath her covers, she repeated, "Human life is precious. Human life is precious. It is inimitable. It is inimitable."

Her voice fell to a whisper as she fell asleep. Just as she passed the veil of consciousness, she forgot her words and slurred her sleepy speech. The mantra morphed. "Life is inevitable. Life is inevitable."

A storm came while Zara slept. As it raged, so too did she, for there were no happy dreams. Only nightmares.

She dreamed her baby was wrapped in her arms. It was not crying. It made no sound at all. So, she unwrapped the blanket, and unwrapped it some more. And more. And more! It was an endless cocoon, one which she frantically flayed in search for her child.

For days it seemed she searched, ripping layer upon layer of cloth from the infinite wrap. Until, at last, she gave up.

She let out a hopeless wail and sank to her knees. She bowed her head and at that moment, the blankets unfurled. She had uncovered it.

It. Not the child. The child had disappeared, replaced by a haunting void. It seemed to be watching her. When she tilted her gaze, the void seemed to blink.

Zara tried to speak to it, to ask for her child. This was a mistake. The void rushed forth in torrents. It entered her mouth, gagging her with shadow. Her eyes widened in terror. These too were blinded by blackness. Everything went dark.

Finally, in the bleak nothing, she heard her baby's cry. It was just ahead, in a viscous layer of shadow. Zara called to the child. Her voice was muted by some other power. She ran toward the baby, climbing down silent steps that made no echo. All the while, the baby's scream grew quieter and quieter. Down she went, calling in vain to a child that could not hear her. She went to the very pits of the void, where there was nothing except the pressure of many leagues above her.

It was then she felt, somehow, that she knew this empty pit. It was her womb.

The weight of all above now bore upon her breast. One last time, she screamed. One last time, she made a noise. But it was not her own. It belonged to a boy, distorted and dampened. The child's cry oozed out of her mouth and slipped away into nothingness.

Thunder crashed; Zara shot upright. Rain clanked on the roof like beggars clinking for alms. She looked around. The courtyard glistened with carpets of raindrops. Ponds formed beneath clogged gutters. Flashes of light scattered off the slippery stone, refracting into brief glimpses of an ephemeral night sky.

She liked thunderstorms. They were rowdy, as her neighbors had been. They were bright, like her father's smile. And most importantly, they kept her company in the lonely nights, as her husband had done. Zara flashed a look at her belly and waited for a kicking that had stopped weeks ago.

"You don't have to be a kicker," she told the child. She glanced at the crib; Al had messed it up. Zara went to tidy it, ignoring the flaming pain in her cervix. She creased the wrinkles on the blanket, restacked her childhood toys neatly in the corner, and returned to bed—fleetingly contented.

For a while, she listened to the water stampeding off the roof. It kept her distracted from her aching abdominals and creeping nausea. Moreover, it kept her noisy thoughts at bay until they too became torrential. Then, a flash illuminated the Tulou. Thunder followed, quaking with the complaints of some derelict god. The crackling muted her worry for a moment. Then, that too began to quake.

Zara shivered and moaned. She heaved into her puke bucket. Her hair fell in front of her mouth and was coated in vomit. "Uhngh," she moaned. She stared into the bucket and gagged some more. She retched until there was nothing left to expel but noxious air. She stared at her soaked, stringy hair. Her husband would have held it for her. Al would have, too. She moaned again, louder; so the ghosts could hear.

The simple fact was she was lonely. And if that was a crime, so be it. It was a human one. Yet, it was this business of oh-so-human crimes that bothered Zara. For if Al had been a Puritan, his mistake would have been just that: a mistake, born only out of naivety and empathy. Two of the noblest qualities.

And that, much to Zara's chagrin, was the issue she found herself mulling over. The singular truth she kept hiding from beneath her covers. The lone fact that kept her company when her hair dangled into the bucket.

Al had poisoned her, yes. He had harmed her child, true. But he had also shown her how truly frail she was. How precariously her pregnancy teetered. And most of all, how dark her days had been.

And so she sat, cocooned within her covers, thinking up excuses for the strange automaton's mistake.

"Al is a child, at least in mind." (She said this aloud, for of course the walls have ears). "He has a man's face but he was never born! Not until one day, his electronics misfired and made him... Whatever he is."

She declared in an argumentative tone—one rarely used for inanimate objects— "He is a stowaway in an automaton's body. A man immaculately conceived."

After saying so, Zara listened. Though, she knew not for what. A sign, perhaps. Some wayward metaphor she could take and use for her own purpose. But none came. Not yet.

She let out a staccato breath and got to her feet. Once again, she tidied the crib, this time placing the toys in a different corner. "Do you like it, my son? I made the green blankie special for you. It was your father's favorite color."

Zara wiped the corners of her eyes. "It's okay to be quiet. I was shy, too. That's okay." She patted the old wood of the crib and eyed her bed. With nothing but sweaty blankets and worries to keep her warm, sleeping was becoming a moot point. So, she grabbed her coat. If she was going to mull about, she might as well pray.

However, the Ancestral Hall was soaked. The brazier was extinguished. Puddles like a moat surrounded the shrine. Rather than return indoors—where ghosts and worse awaited her—she walked through the sheltered circumference of the courtyard, thinking. After several soaking laps, she began to shiver. Only then did she pay heed to her body.

A body that was increasingly breaking down. Al may have been wrong about her child. He may have been impulsive. But he was right about one thing. She was dying. Zara knew that to be true. And she had sent away the only soul that would show her any kindness.

Which is why, in the end, she went to the crypts to cry.

14

METAPHORS AND SIGNS

Zara woke beside her husband's coffin. Her nose was runny. Her eyes were tender and puffy. She sighed, "Sorry for disturbing you, baby." It was not the first time she had broken down before the dead.

Sleeping in the crypts had worsened her aches. Her legs were stiff and her eyesight was blurry. Worse, she had the most annoying sniffles, the kind that dripped like a liquid and could not be stopped with a sneeze.

When she came to the surface, there was no smog in the sky. It was brighter than any day in recent memory. It took time for her eyes to adjust. When they did, the first thing she saw was a mockingbird.

Now, for the typical person, this might have meant little. At best, they might recall a past memory. Indeed, that is what occurred with Zara. She remembered the poem she wrote with Al. But that was not all. Zara was a Puritan. Everything had a double or triple meaning. And that mockingbird was not just happenstance. It was a messenger.

One that, for now, Zara only blinked at. The light was giving her a headache and that would only make her more nauseous.

She focused on reviving the Ancestral Flame. The shrine was built with drainage in mind and was already dry in the full sun. So too was the woodpile, which was stacked atop the rafters. And yet, as Zara reached for fresh kindling, she realized it was not needed. The flame had rekindled itself.

The Puritan stared in wonder. She had seen the brazier last night. The torrents had quenched it. Now, it had somehow come back to life. Zara leaned forward. Had someone else come to light it? The thought excited her. Had Al returned?

She splashed through puddles of standing water and entered her room. As usual, it was empty. Nonetheless, she went back to the courtyard, scouring the mud for clues. There were the typical prints: rats, deer, rabbits, and even a dog. No footprints, though. Her gaze settled back on the brazier. It truly had relit itself.

Zara pondered the situation during her morning prayers. While reciting the litany of ancestors, she peered into the flame as if it were a mirror. And if that seems strange, one must remember that metaphor is infinite. Symbolism can be found wherever it is looked for. Faces can be found in fallen leaves. Words can be heard on the wind. And signs for desperate souls—those appear in abundance.

Zara finished the litany and fell quiet. She swallowed and whispered, so that only the lonesome fire might hear her, "Are autom—is Al really all that bad?"

The fire was quiet. It did not crackle. It did not sway. It was as if it were staring back at her. So, Zara added, "He's different. His mistakes are ones I would make."

The fire was quiet. It did not crackle. It did not sway. Yet, a wind came down from the sky. The fire diminished. Wondering if she had said something displeasing, she added, "Either my child will be the last Puritan, or I will. Would you have it so?"

The wind quieted. The flame grew and gained new life.

Zara contemplated what the fire was saying. Doing so was not hard. The metaphors spilled out as if they were pieces to a puzzle. "Al could care for me until I die. Then, when I am gone—he could raise my child."

The coals crackled angrily.

"Al can be trained in our ways! It would be better than leaving my son on the steps of a heretical orphanage! Or worse, to leave the last of us for feral dogs!"

Another gust came. Again, the flame shrank. It did not grow again. Even after Zara fetched fresh logs and fanned the flame. This rather obvious metaphor made her frown. Clearly, the ancestors thought she was double-dipping.

Defeated and despairing, Zara slunk back to her bedroom. She changed into fresh clothes, choosing her favorite blue dress. If she were not pregnant, it would be far too big on her. But that was why she liked it. It was roomy and breathable. She patted her belly and smiled, "Good morning, little man."

Silence.

"Are you hungry?"

Silence.

"Just one kick? Just a little nudge to let mommy know you're listening?"

The only noise was a growl coming from her empty stomach.

Zara took a long, deep breath and wiped away a tear. More painful than her aches and pains was the pit forming in her heart. She wiped away another tear and smiled hopefully, "I bet you're just hungry."

She went to the refrigerator, trying to ignore the hum of the chiller fan. She stared morosely at the heathen-grown food. So used to game and sickly crops, the full bounty was unbelievable and overwhelming. She salivated. Heretically modified or not, it all looked delicious.

Zara was not much of a cook, though. Even when she was healthier, her husband had been the chef. She snacked on what was immediately edible: carrots, sliced cheese, lab-grown salt squares that made her cheeks pop.

Thus began a cycle of periodically going to the fridge, staring at it expectantly, and settling for what she had already had too many bites of. Then, she would take the scraps to her bed and nibble on them until the cycle repeated.

In a word, she scavenged. At one point, she did get creative. She melted butter on a piece of bread and coated it in tomato sauce. It was as appetizing as it sounds and... She ate an entire loaf this way.

Somewhat full (and entirely sick to her stomach), Zara dusted the crumbs off her sheets. In doing so, she reprimanded herself for not eating at the table. She glanced at the dining area and shrugged.

Then, she did a double-take. The Puritan Annals were open. Zara tilted her head, trying to remember if she had left it so. That did not seem likely, as she always closed it to protect the yellowing pages. Moreover, the Annals were heavy. Stray gusts could never have opened the book on their own.

That left happenstance as the only explanation. But to Zara, whose mind was cultivated on prophecy and providence, this seemed like another sign. One which the Puritan craved more than any food.

She sat and studied the open page. It was part of the middle sections, written after gene-editing became the norm but before it took its toll on the Pure Folk. Like most of the middle entries, this was a poem Zara had never read. The middling years were very contentious among the Pure Folk, full of fringe ideas and dangerous divisions.

Not only had the page been ripped out and rebound several times—the writing had been effaced and rewritten as well. The original poem was a blackened stump in the center of the page. A copy was scribbled into the margins.

The only true ism is schism
The last human shall never die
The first was never born
A thing changes
Human being ranges
Hear no talk of Human

Zara reread the poem. Then, she read it aloud. Each word weeded the anxiety from her heart. Its message was like rain to dried clay. She swelled as she embraced it. Then, she started to doubt herself again. This could all just be random. Meaningless.

Like a toddler before a cookie jar, she said innocently, "Just one more." She flipped to the next page, eyes pinched shut. She prayed that all would be resolved and make sense, that the mockingbird and the brazier were messages after all. "Just one more sign."

She opened her eyes and peered down at the page. Her jaw dropped.

The page was blank.

15

THE PAGE UNWRITTEN

Zara searched for hours. She had hoped Al was spying on her again, that once she left the Tulou, he would run back to her. When that did not happen, she assumed he had left the Steel Swamp.

Reluctantly, she made her way to the Fractal Span. It was a soulless piece of infrastructure. One whose twisted geometry was enough to make her dizzy. But beyond just hating the bridge for philosophical reasons, she was also afraid of heights.

Zara stared down the length of the Span. There was a slight wind, causing the bridge to creak and sway. Two things bridges ought not do, in her opinion. She coiled her pale hands around the railing and reminded herself that she had recently made this crossing. *Just the other day, when I first met Al and that doctor.*

"Come on, Zara. It's just a walk. Just a casual stroll with a small likelihood of falling to your death. No different than getting out of bed, really. Save for the distance."

She took her first step. Then, her second. Soon, she had taken a dozen. Yet, when she heard the distorted sound of the water below, she unconsciously looked down. The ocean's maw gaped at her. Its saltwater tongue lapped against limestone teeth.

Zara froze in terror. She stayed suspended on the Span for several minutes, unable and then unwilling to move. Were it not for her righteous zeal (and a great deal of adrenaline), she would have turned around. Eventually, though, she found the willpower to ignore her fears. She looked straight ahead, tuned out the water, and sped down the final portion of the bridge.

Finally, she entered the residential borough. It was a mausoleum of steel and glass, one Zara rarely saw up close or in broad daylight. Now in full sun, she saw the city in all its neck-kinking glory. The skyscrapers were tall, shiny, and immaculate. No stains on the windows, no bends to their beams. Perfect, in their own corrupt way.

The humans were much the same. Marble skin, chiseled jaws, carven extremities... They looked like statues escaped from a museum. And as Zara threaded her way through the cluttered streets, she felt like an animal escaped from the zoo. She bowed her head, afraid of engaging with the tall, shiny mutants.

She found a nice park bench and sat there for a while, observing and feeling observed. Kids without manners pointed at her and asked questions. Adults with manners did the same. This caused her to sweat nervously.

The sooner you find Al, she told herself, *the sooner you can leave.* She flagged down her first mutant.

"Excuse me, sir! Have you seen an automaton walking around here? He's rather handsome. For an automaton, of course! No wrinkles. Like you, actually. Uh... anyways, he's about my height. Dark hair. Not really hair, though. I think it's not hair. Hey, where are you going?"

She had scared him off. Or perhaps he was in a hurry. Or, he was bad-mannered. Either way, Zara continued undeterred.

"Excuse me..."

"Yes, pardon me, bu—"

"Sir, do you—"

Nobody would listen to her. They were not accustomed to having frank conversations with strangers. Moreover, to the general population, Zara was quite ugly. She was short, her nose was too big, and her breasts were too small. She had one freckle too many and one forehead injection too few. This perceived inadequacy made most people view Zara as untrustworthy.

Finally, a young girl stopped.

"Yes, little girl. Hello! Have you seen an automaton walking around these parts? He'd seem dejected. Kind of human, almost."

The girl blinked, in awe of Zara's chromatic pupils, those opals inset in eyeballs. She asked, confused, "You lost your servant?"

The girl's mother tugged at her, "Come on, honey. This woman is clearly sick."

Zara lunged after them, snot leaking down her nose. "Yes. Have you seen him?"

The girl asked her mother, "Do some automatons not have trackers?"

"They all do, honey," the mother replied, hoisting the child up and shuffling off. "That woman is loony, that's all."

Of course, Zara realized. She was asking as if Al was human! But Al was made to be property. To be owned. She did not need to waste words on heathen mutants! All she had to do was talk to that damned doctor!

Yes, every automaton is implanted with a tracking chip. Thus, Doctor Fusselquark did not worry about dear Al. That was, until he noticed something odd. For almost a week, the automaton had been hiving around the Puritan village. Aside from a brief excursion south, the automaton had remained near the northern coast. Then one day, the automaton went south again.

At first, the doctor thought this was due to the Puritan woman. Perhaps she was taking him on a hike. Unbothered, Doctor Fusselquark went to bed and had pleasant dreams about the apocalypse.[1]

In the morning, Fusselquark rolled off the couch. He chugged a happiness tonic to ward off his nihilism. Then, he walked over to his workstation and checked on the grand experiment.

"Hm," he hummed. "Still not updating the location." He refreshed the software and rebooted his computer. When that failed, Fusselquark accessed the automaton's data backups. The last update had taken place the night prior. He extracted the file and accessed the recent footage. The videos were condensed, with artificial intelligence showing only the valuable bits.

So it was that Doctor Fusselquark learned of his automaton's escapades.

He muttered as he feverishly typed his notes, "The boy's in love. And the girl, I'll be damned—she tolerates it!"

...

"Puritan Annals," Fusselquark jotted onto his pad. "Ah, yes. Three tenets. Very aesthetically pleasing."

...

The Chief Scientist heard all the important parts of Al's story, even the mockingbird poem. "Marvellous," he stated, circling something he had written earlier. He sat back and massaged his chin, "What a sappy, heartfelt pile of slop!"

Then came the last portion of the recordings. At this point, the footage began flickering, buffering, and skipping.

---

[1]. To you or me, these would have been nightmares. To the doctor, whose mind was regularly disturbed, it was Tuesday.

It became more like a comic book of individual pictures. Fusselquark observed Zara's scowl, a bronze spear, a courtyard, and a smokestack. He had to slow the recording to piece the slide show together. He noted in his log, "Emotional distress affecting cognition?"

Fusselquark leaned back in his chair. He rewatched the footage up to the point of Al's exile. As the recording went on, his expression grew sullen. The experiment was teetering toward collapse just as it was getting interesting. He grumbled, "This is hardly enough for a white paper, let alone my magnum opus." He found an ampule of toxic chemicals with which to fidget. He tossed it about haphazardly, chewing on the tactile cap in concentration. "The experiment must continue..."

The doctor could not simply move Al back to the Tulou. Good science is observed, not ordained. He mocked the very idea, "Yes, hello—dying woman in a superstitious cult? Would you mind keeping my automaton so that I might have complete notes? Please and thank you."

"No, that won't do. They must make their choices themselves..."

And make them they did. When Fusselquark heard the bell in his lobby, he nearly bit the ampule between his teeth. Then, seeing who had come in, he spat it right out. He exclaimed, "Darwin's grave! What luck!"

The lobby smelled damp and musky like a wet dog. Zara supposed the smell was due to the tower's old foundation, or water damage from the recent rains. She rang the bell in the lobby, waited for a few minutes, and when the doctor did not emerge, rang it again. Repeatedly. Emphatically. Insistently.

The doctor stumbled out from the laboratory, still putting on his white coat. He forgot to adjust the collar and it remained fashionably popped. "Have you changed your mind?" Fusselquark asked, fumbling for his pocket scanner.

"In one regard," Zara answered. "Not in the one you suggest."

"A pity," Fusselquark tutted his tongue. "Then why have you come?"

"Your automaton. It has been annoying me."

"I've not seen him," the doctor replied innocently.

"Because he's gone and fallen in love with me."

The doctor laughed. "A machine? I seriously doubt it." He leaned over the lobby desk. "You religious types always read too much into things."

Zara put her hands on her hips, "He has fixed my refrigerator, cooked me meals, and written me poetry. Trust me, your little darling-bot thinks he's in love."

"Then why is he not beside you?" Fusselquark questioned.

Zara did not reply, as she would rather not get into any specifics. She was not overly proud of her behavior. She had fallen for and quarreled with a calculator. And while she could see the nuance in her situation, a stranger would not.

Fusselquark looked her up and down, "I presume you've lost my property, then?"

"I'm not the one who gave a computer legs," Zara retorted.

"And I am not the one who gave him a heart."

Zara scoffed, "He has no heart... He's just been reading too much poetry."

The doctor chuckled, "I don't doubt that." He got up and opened the door to his laboratory. "Please," he gestured.

After a moment's hesitation, Zara followed.

He led her to a sunken couch with too many blotches to be counted as stains. "Make yourself comfortable. Tea?"

"No thanks," Zara replied. "We should not drink in a laboratory, right?"

"Eh," the doctor shrugged. "Most of these chemicals end up in your water supply anyway. At least here they're concentrated enough to give you a buzz."

Zara could not tell if he was joking. Either way, she did not appreciate his sense of humor, nor the smell of sausage coming from one of his instruments. "Do you cook your breakfast in that thing?"

"Oh yes," he patted the tan box proudly, "Better than a microwave, a gas chromatograph."

"Lovely. Anyway..." She muttered as if she did not care for an answer, "You can find your, uh, *thing*, then?"

"Oh, yes." Fusselquark flicked on a monitor. He pointed to a red dot on a blue map. "Been there about two days. I thought he was off trying to write another poem." He flashed a coy look at her and then snorted, "Simulacrum!"

He's heard the poem. What else might he have heard? She blushed and wrapped her arms around her breasts. *Or seen?*

The doctor grabbed two coffee mugs hanging on hooks near the X-ray diffractometer. "Still a 'no' on refreshments?"

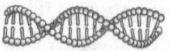

Tea was served in Fusselquark's penthouse. It was surprisingly archaic, with wooden paneling, peeling paint, and a nice, antique smell. "What an interesting home you have."

"The better to die in," the doctor smiled.

Zara cocked her brow. With nothing to say to that, she reached for a peach.

"Oh, my apologies. Those are purely decorative."

"Of course they are," Zara grumbled. "How is it possible?"

"Plastic, mostly."

"No, not the fruit. How could an automaton, a machine, fall in love?"

"Tripping…" Fusselquark began before immediately trailing off on a tangential thought. He resumed after a pause. "What was I saying? Ah, yes. Tripping is not an intended design. It comes about from having legs. Choking is not an intended design, either. It comes as a result of needing to eat and breathe." He sipped his tea, "Love may be similar. An unintentional effect of complex programming."

Zara drank her tea. It was very bitter, though with a nice aftertaste. "You don't talk like a scientist. You know that?"

"Good. Most of my peers are an embarrassment to the profession. Flagellating themselves with sheets of data and proclaiming themselves enlightened."

Zara chuckled, "You would have made a decent Puritan."

Fusselquark agreed. "Good science, when done strictly, is not too dissimilar from religion."

"Science," Zara rolled her eyes. "Science is a mockery of life."

The Chief Scientist of Panacea sipped his tea.

Zara eyed him, "You disagree."

Fusselquark set down his cup and added another sugar cube. Then, another and another. "Not at all. We are a people in stasis, suspended in the idyllic debauchery of a scientific age. An age we no longer deserve." He took another sip of his tea and nodded to himself.

Zara stared at the doctor. He was just as odd as his automaton. Almost likable. She inquired, "Is this tea okay to drink while pregnant?"

"Are you feeling unwell?"

"No worse than yesterday," Zara lied.

The doctor leaned forward in his chair and squinted at her face. He shook his head, "You have a cold."

"Perhaps I do," Zara shrugged. She quietly chastised herself for pacing in the rain.

"I could give you some medication? Your people are not the most tolerant of disease."

"Because you've gone and made the whole island one mutant zoo!" She asked again, emphasizing every word, "Is this tea okay for a pregnant Puritan to drink?"

Fusselquark would have liked to give the woman a few preemptive medications. Puritans were notoriously frail. He sighed, not wanting to further interfere with his experiment. "Perfectly safe. How are the pregnancy pains?"

"Good," Zara replied. "Better today, actually. Though... I did think I was going into labor yesterday. It turned out to be a mistake, but I do wonder. Could—Could I give birth this early?"

"It's not unheard of. Without a trained technologist, I doubt your baby would survive." Fusselquark cleared his throat, "But I'm sure you want a natural birth. Whatever that means."

"I do," Zara nodded.

"Very well." Fusselquark took a deep breath that, upon exhaling, seemed to drain him of his energy. He looked out a north-facing window, "Al is near the Wasteworks. Beside a canal, I suspect."

"Can you tell him to return?"

"To whom?" the doctor asked.

Zara glared at him.

Fusselquark chuckled grimly, "I only joke." He walked toward a corner of the hall and looked down at a jumbled mess of maps. He lied, "I have tried to ping him. He will not come."

"He won't? How is that possible? Don't all your little machines come when they are called?"

"They do," acknowledged the doctor. "But I believe his glitch has made him human... All too human."

THE LITTLE AI THAT COULD (BUT SHOULDN'T)

The Wasteworks were a foul and oozy place, a dumping ground for defective robots. Not the best place for a reunion, but Al had not intended to be found. He had claimed a lonely heap and climbed atop it. Now, he waited on the assembly line of death, waiting for his chance to be recycled.

Zara found him with his body curled in a tight, power-saving mode, high atop a mound of metal. He looked like a child in fetal position. A blue light faintly emanated from his ocular sensor. "Al?"

The automaton did not move.

While Zara may have lived without automation all her life, she was not entirely ignorant. She pulled him down from the mound and put him on his back. She unhooked the section of plastic that concealed his chest cavity, unscrewed the finger-tight connections, and peered at the automaton's innards.

Sure enough, the battery light blinked orange. Zara looked at her surroundings. An eternal smog floated over the towering recycling centers. The only colors that penetrated the haze were red, crimson, and occasionally scarlet.

It was not enough to feed his micro-solar panels. Zara shut his chest cavity. She hoisted the heavy automaton upright. The knees activated automatically, clicking mechanically into a linear pose.

Unfortunately, that made it difficult to transport him (automatons were built to carry people, not the other way around). She could have returned to the Tulou and used a dolly, but the terrain was hilly with the barrows of long-forgotten scrap. So, she fashioned a rope from the fibrous cables of a large, robotic arm. Wrapping the cables once around her waist, she then tied the ends around Al's wrists.

She took a step. The cable tautened, pulling Al flat onto his face. Zara sighed. She had not thought about that. His pretty face would be dragged through the mud. She glanced back at him, "Scrapes and smudges suit you better anyway."

She set off through the Steel Swamp, dragging the automaton behind her. She went up shifting silicone dunes and down valleys of stratified scrap. She ambled across beaches of sedimented batteries and plodded through polymer thickets. When the opportunity presented itself, she used the borough's automation to her benefit. She rode leviathan arms over factory yards, hoboed on steel, serpentine streams, and hitchhiked a time on a golem's high head.

All the while, Zara struggled with Al's weight. She hacked and heaved the entire way. When she chanced upon a stretch of dappled sunlight on the banks of a petroleum pond, she had to take a break. Yet as she caught her breath beneath the muted rays, she noticed she was not getting warm. Nor were her boogers going away. Her cold was worsening.

It was here that Zara ignored the animal instinct of self-preservation. She ignored the signs of her oncoming illness and continued pulling Al back to the Tulou. Every strained step, she pictured her baby's crib. And in that picture, Al was beside it with a bottle.

"Just a mile more," she began to say when she was several miles off.

After many stops to hack up globs of phlegm, to catch her fleeting breath, and to nurse her aching body, she finally returned to the Tulou. Exhausted and feverish, she left him on the steps of the Ancestral Hall, where the afternoon sun could charge him back up. Meanwhile, she gathered all the blankets she could find and shambled to bed for a long sleep.

16

THE MOMENT THAT TOOK AN EON

OFTEN, THE PASSAGE OF time is slow and change is a creeping, distant reality. However, an entire eon can also occur in a moment, as when an asteroid paves the future with the bones of dinosaurs. Such shifts need not be destructive, though. Sometimes, they are as small as a cell or as insignificant as a fallen stone.

On a humid summer morning, such a shift occurred. It came without fanfare or warning, as is the cosmos' custom. The universe never begins a new epoch by sending out invitations.

Al was recharged at dawn. His sensors blinked in the early morning light. His internals performed a brief diagnostic scan. His archives booted up, his fans began to hum, and he gradually became aware of his surroundings.

The Tulou... How did I get here? The last thing he had seen was the fading light of a sanguine moon. The last thing he had felt was the chill of an empty battery. There was no way for him to have gotten back here, especially on his own. The only way for him to be there was to have been brought.

Zara? He questioned. He performed another analysis as the warming rays hit his micro-solar panels. There was a statistical likelihood that the doctor had placed him here. His owner had an insatiable scientific curiosity, especially regarding Al's newfound behaviors. Nonetheless, Al did not think the doctor was responsible. Fusselquark would never tamper with an experiment.

Al scanned his recent files for clues as to what had happened. His short-term storage did indeed have recent uploads. He opened one of the files, expecting to see a recording of events. Instead, he got a fragmented, poorly resolved set of pictures. He could make out little. Luckily, the pictures were in sequence. He saw Zara staring at his chest cavity. Then, a makeshift rope. Later, Zara braced herself at the knees and coughed. Finally, he saw her leaving him at this exact point and going to her room.

That left the answer apparent. Zara had changed her mind. She had taken him back.

The automaton began to rock back and forth. The many facets of his algorithmic wit struggled to understand the situation. He had displeased Zara. He had gone away to please her. Had that displeased her? Was she happy with him now? He reflected on the data.

Perhaps she wanted to scrap me herself?

His wit countered with the obvious. *She would not have let you recharge.*

Again, he found a counterargument. *She may not know how I produce energy.*

Al looked at Zara's door. None of the traps were armed. Still, he did not want to enter uninvited. As words sometimes function as doorbells, he awed in a fake, overly sentimental voice, "Home..."

Al turned an audio receptor toward Zara's door, anticipating that the woman would now come out. Still, there was nothing. Luckily, patience was an easy virtue to program in a machine, even one so unique as Al. He sat on the steps of the shrine and stared at Zara's apartment.

Despite a cloud of pollution settling above the ringed village, the Tulou was peaceful and quiet. There was no wind that morning until a lone gust penetrated the stone walls. It was a short and wild wind that rolled through the Tulou. It mischievously hit Zara's door before snickering off. As it did, it pushed the door open.

Al stared into her dark chambers. "Zara?"

He received no response. He hesitated, hoping for an invitation that increasingly seemed unlikely. The *tip-tap* of a leaking gutter became like the *tick-tock* of a clock. For Al, time was soon measured in anxious thoughts.

"Are you asleep?" He asked, louder.

Tip-tap.

"Zara?" Al asked again, louder still.

Something was wrong. Zara needed his help. Yet, help was precisely the thing he was scared to offer. He could not trust his directives any longer. Not after the Pinon Root debacle. So, he waited—perhaps too long, when all was said and done. But wait he did, until finally the full moon began to rise above the Tulou. Only then did Al approach the apartment.

At first, he intended only to shut the door and resume his watch. Yet, his particulate monitors noted a peculiar scent from within—a subtle mix of spoiled fish, moldy cheese, and bad breath. Kind of like how humans always smell, only more so. Curious, Al entered Zara's room. He noted another smell instantly: candlewax and lavender. It came from several candles near Zara's bed. These had been lit many hours ago and flickered dimly at wick's end.

Zara held her book of poems at her breast. Al smiled at her, hoping the gesture would miraculously wake her up (as was the case in many human stories). But this was not a human story, and Zara did not wake.

Al crept quietly to her side. Her face was tranquil, though paler than he remembered. It had all the markings of an intricate life, frown lines intersecting with smile lines. Crow's feet blurred with bags under the eyes. Al stared like a patron in an art museum. He savored the upward curl of her brow, the furl of her upper lip. He put to eternal memory the constellated freckles of her cheeks. Craving to see the light in her opaline eyes, he nudged her.

The book of poems slid off her chest. "Apologies," he whispered, retrieving the journal. It was opened to an enscribbled page. Al studied the poem. It was the one she had read to him, so many days ago. Now, it was finished. He squinted at the text, figuring out which word was meant to go where from the lineouts and words in the margins.

> *There is a phrase that bids farewell,*
> *Said softly at the door.*
> *Seeing off the severed halves*
> *Of a soul that daily splinters.*
>
> *This often-uttered oath*
> *Of three words thickly woven*
> *Is a wreath to warm the heart*
> *That each day is doomed to part.*
>
> *Not a sentence, but a spell;*
> *A ward against a world of harm,*
> *A knot to keep the cord of fate*
> *Wrapped 'round us one more day.*
>
> *Yet, time's a rising tide*
> *And we are footsteps in the sand.*
> *The Ferryman finds us all,*
> *No matter what our plans.*
>
> *That is why this wreath*
> *Is hung daily at the door.*

Not mere words we wish to say,
But a soul's return to sender.

And presented with those words
That a thousand times have thatched
The leaky roof of love,
Death will hand us each a horn.

As we board his golden boat
At the harborage of the heart,
He'll have us hold up to the ear
The horn and then we'll hear:

A countless lovers' choir sing
Those same words as they were
When the universe awoke and wept
And wove itself a wife.

The horizon hoists its anchor.
The shoreline of life will fade.
But the Ferryman will know where to,
He'll hear the song of me and you.

Just then, Al noticed it was very quiet. Not even a whistle came from Zara as she slept. The automaton rose and stared at her chest.

Eons happen sometimes in moments; yet sometimes, moments take eons. Al waited ages for the woman's chest to rise and fall. He locked his senses in stasis, yearning for a soft breath or slight movement.

Nothing.

His algorithms failed him. He froze. Data processors stalled as his archives refused to update. Every command lagged. His arm clanked and his hand clinked. Trembling, he touched Zara. Her cold arm fell to the side of the bed.

17

HEAR NO TALK OF HUMAN

ALL A HUMAN'S LIFE is spent learning how to die. They get rather good at it. Some use religion, others find solace in their deeds. Still others shrug off mortality and enjoy every moment. Regardless of their methods, one thing is absolutely certain: humans are very good at grieving. They grieve for family, for friends, for pets. They even grieve for past places and times, though they call this nostalgia and consider it rather enjoyable.

Al had no such preparation. No automaton was meant to grieve because none were meant to feel. The weight of loss was one of the few burdens never meant for artificial intelligence. Yet, on that bleak summer's night, Al's algorithms began coiling and constricting themselves. His intellect had been built on logic and datasets. No code or script could process this new sensation. He had no preparation—only facts.

And facts do little to quell grief.

He prepared for Zara's burial. First, he built a makeshift casket by dismantling the dining table and bed frame. The final touches came from the baby's would-be crib. He used that for the lid. Next, he dusted the sconces, gathered what candles remained about the Tulou, and lit the crypts as best he could. Due to the recent rains, much of the underground was underwater. This Al could not abide. He found an old shovel and dug out a portion of mud from the corners of the tomb, constructing a crudely fashioned berm at the end of the hall. This was his last necessary task. The rest—and there were many—were an active form of idling. Pure procrastination. They served only to delay the inevitable.

Finally, Al gathered Zara in his arms and brought her to the crypts. The claystone walls had swelled, and chunks of rock fell like flowers strewn before a procession. They fell first into stony pools of standing water. Then, in the newer section, they pitter-pattered into muddy pits before piling up at the end of the hall. There, atop an earthen mound already sinking, sat the caskets of Pierre and Zara Attrush.

Al stared at her ramshackle tomb. It seemed such a poor home for such a rich human. Al held her close to his chest, unable to let go. He stood there for hours, a mortuary statue. He neither moved, spoke, swayed, nor sobbed—nor could he have even if he had wanted to. And that was the worst pain of all. He felt all the pain of a human but had no way to express it. There was no heart to ache, no metabolism to make him shiver, nor any tear ducts with which to cry. Just a sickening grief that boiled in a lidded pot.

Zara began to bloat. Her face swelled and became hard to look upon. Only then—and with great difficulty—did Al lay her to rest. He placed her on her side, so that she and her husband could look at one another forever. He closed the casket and left the crypts, blowing each candle out as he went. And though he could not shed a tear, the weeping mud rained onto her wooden tomb. It echoed like a drum.

Outside, the Ancestral Shrine was gloomy and quiet. The brazier's flame was only a memory. Al entered the hall and stared at the ashes. A few lively embers remained. Strangely, they took on a new life to Al, those lamps in an ashen void. They became a symbol, a piece of living poetry. He thought about how, if there was an afterlife, Zara might be happy if he kept the fire burning.

The automaton added kindling and blew on the embers. Like a drowning man gasping for breath, flames burst forth. The heat of the brazier warmed Al's mainframe. He savored the sensation on his cheeks. He relished the firelight, reveling in its whiplike motions. Then, he did something strange. Perhaps it was out of superstition, perhaps it was out of respect. Or, maybe a grieving supercomputer behaves oddly. At any rate, he said aloud, "For one more day, Zara's flame will burn on."

Al bowed his head and observed a moment of silence. However, in the silence his statement echoed. Every time it did so, it mutated, metamorphosing into a metaphor. A metaphor unlike any he had ever thought. It hit him with the impact of a thousand meteors. Al blinked at the brazier. There were coals that need not cool and embers left to kindle.

He rushed back into the crypt.

The Technolithic Tower was empty that day. Al was glad for this. He did not want to confront the Chief Scientist. Not with what he was about to do.

The automaton entered the laboratory and placed Zara on the base-blender. Al frowned at her once-perfect face. The rigor mortis was getting the best of her features, tautening her grand wrinkles. Al touched her chilled brow. "All you need is the proper kindling."

He got a kit of tools and took out a surgical knife. He made several careful incisions through her limbs, her neck, and eventually—her chest. The chilled blood oozed out and began to soak the machine. Al had to hurry. He sprinted to an old cabinet of maintenance parts. From there, he took a chromatographic pump, a handful of narrow, stainless-steel capillaries, a xenon lamp, and several miscellaneous circuit boards.

These he fixed together into a new sort of machine. Not quite a heart, not quite lungs. Not quite biological, not quite mechanical. It was very much a theoretical design. And very illegal. The soldering took several hours, the tinkering several more. In the end, the artificial organ resembled something halfway between a brain and motherboard.

Al implanted the apparatus into Zara's chest. Then, as he stared at her innards, specifically her noxious womb, he was suddenly inspired. He made an incision below her stomach and gathered another set of parts.

Al devised a similar implant for Zara's malformed fetus. It had died shortly before Zara but was nonetheless salvageable. He almost ran out of capillary tubing by the end. Thankfully, he had just enough to create a second, more specialized device. One that could grow and adapt in vivo. When he was finished, he stared at his work with a sense of pride.

If successful, not only would Zara return to him, she and her child would be far healthier than any human. They might even be like him.

The thought made Al giddy. He quickly stitched Zara back up and began sifting through the laboratory glassware. He opened cabinets and compartments, broke ampules of rare chemicals, and transferred them to volumetric flasks. Then, he diluted the concoction and filled three syringes. Ever a slave to procedure, Al put a chemical hazards sticker on the formulation and circled all but the 'health-hazard' pictogram. Finally, he acquired the most important reagent.

Without it, the base-blender would not just malfunction—it might well blow up.

Al approached the chemical cabinet and delicately measured out 50 milliliters of apple juice. He loaded it into the excipient compartment.

Now came the hard part. The taboo part. The most certainly illegal and quite possibly most heinous act in history part. It was time to rewrite some code. Biological and otherwise.

Al had prepared to be on this step for many hours—days, if necessary. He had anticipated some firewall to protect against what he was about to do. Indeed, there was one, but it was mostly to protect against curious scientists or wayward laypeople. The jumbled mess of digital vaults and locks were no match for an independent automaton. After a few million iterations, he had cracked the code and broken into the firmware of the base-blender. After that, all Al needed to do was change a few ones to zeros. And like that, it was done.

The way to immortality was open.

The automaton looked one last time at Zara's corpse and turned to the control panel. He pressed the big, red button. The blender hummed. The belt began moving. Zara's bloated, sewn-up body disappeared behind a burst of steam. The chromium doors locked into place.

Al paced back and forth, never taking his oculars off those doors. He sucked in his lips as if he had eaten something sour. He rubbed his hands together like he was starting a fire. As the seconds became minutes, his impatience turned to worry.

The laboratory was getting warm. The base-blender was not just humming now; it was groaning and grinding. *Clink! Clink! Clink!*

Al had hoped it would subside. Instead, the machine started shaking and smoking. Sparks flew out the back of the blender. Inside the chamber, an exothermic reaction shattered the syringes one by one. *Snap! Snap! Snap!*

Then, surprisingly—everything grew still and silent. Al craned his neck, eyeing the machine suspiciously. Had it worked? Was it over? He took a step toward the base-blender. Yet just as he dared to hope, the metal shielding blew off. Shards of glass rained onto Al's head.

He stared in disbelief. The blender was falling apart. The chromium doors began to warp and bend before finally, the system over-pressurized. The base-blender suddenly shut down. Its modules blinked red in error. The control panel went into error mode.

Beep! Beep! Beep!

Al approached and peeked through the crack in the doors. He saw nothing. He tried to pull them open, but the doors had warped around each other and were stuck. Not even a crowbar was any help. He sat back at the control panel and bowed his head in contemplation. He had failed.

Beep! Beep! Beep!

Al turned off the alarm. He needed silence to think. The first thing he had to do was retrieve Zara's body. Every idle moment risked further decay. He would have to heat the doors just enough to separate them. Once those were removed, he could check on Zara's implants, rebuild the base-blender, and—

Al tilted his head. Something odd had caught his attention. Something... unexpected. Though he had quieted the alarm, the room was not silent. From within the hollow machine came a quiet, repeating hiss. Al squinted, homing in on the sound.

"Not a hiss," he realized. "A breath!"

Al rushed back to the blender and called out to Zara, "This is Al. I am here. Do not be afraid. I will open the doors. I just need to find—"

The gap between the doors widened slightly. The metal whined and compressed. Then, the doors folded in upon themselves. Their leaden weight wrinkled like clothes in the wash. Two, cybernetic hands cast them away like clouds on the wind.

Al gazed at the machine.

Light illuminated the hollow vessel. The various components dangled lifelessly from electric cables. Two eyes looked out from the darkness. Four limbs crawled out from the device.

Zara emerged like an infant from its crib. She looked side to side, squinting at the bright lights. She then saw Al and tilted her head, puzzled.

"Easy," he said warmly. "Take things slow. How do you feel?"

Zara blinked at the massive, metal doors she had just thrown. She opened her mouth to speak and then went quiet. She sat on the edge of the base-blender belt, staring at her forearms with profound confusion. She rotated her wrists, seeing cuts she did not remember getting. She analyzed her bare chest. More cuts. Stitches, too. She leaned forward and stared at her stomach. Out of instinct, she put a hand on it. She jumped, frightened.

"What is it?" Al asked. "Are you still in pain?"

Zara stared at him in horror. She whispered, "A kick."

Al nodded, beaming. "Are you happy? Do you like it?"

Zara's body began to sway. She started to shiver. Her eyes twitched. She looked at Al and back at her belly. She convulsed and collapsed toward the floor.

Al lunged and caught her in his arms. He spoke sweetly, reassuring her that everything was alright now and that she was safe. That only frightened her more.

"A kick!" She gasped.

"Your child is alive," Al encouraged. "Do not be scared! I will take care of you now. Both of you."

Zara looked under the surface of her skin, at a scar that ran across her chest and back. Her confusion melted away when she saw a faint green light where her heart should be. She tried to speak. Her words spilled out as a stutter. She pinched the protruding veins on her forearm. They did not compress.

She tore herself away from the automaton's grasp. She started yelling, but the sight of her scarified body was too much for her. She managed only a few fevered grunts and breathy stammers before fainting back into Al's arms.

The Puritan woke a moment later to the automaton's smile. She wanted to pull away. She wanted to scream. All she could do was weep. And when the tears fell upon her lips, they tasted like metal. "No," she mumbled. "No." She swiveled her head back and forth like a faulty compass, wiping drool on Al's cold chest.

Eons can start in a moment. New eras can be lit with a match. And on that hot summer's evening, on an island halfway between somewhere and nowhere, the future made kindling of the past. And though it came without notice, though it came without fanfare—the new dawn did not begin in silence. It was met with a lament.

"I am a stranger."

Author's Note

Ah, and now we've come to it—the end of the book! I hope that if you have made it this far, you enjoyed this story. If you did not, I commend your perseverance! Regardless of whether you thought it was a classic piece of literature or a piece of something else altogether, please consider leaving a review on Amazon, Goodreads, or wherever else you buy your books. (If you buy your books in person, feel free to scream about the book as you walk down the street.)

The support and *honest* feedback of readers is the most important thing for independent authors. We do not have the luxury of corporate executives telling us our writing sucks. We depend on the charity of our readers for that.

I recommend a palate cleanser after my novels. Something stylistically different or easy to read, like Dr. Seuss or The Bible. If, however, you are not weary of my writing style, below are some novels for your consideration.

The Innkeeper and the Cannibal
The Forlorn Trail: Book 1 of the Eye of Ur
Teo and the Banyan Tree

www.ingramcontent.com/pod-product-compliance
Lightning Source LLC
LaVergne TN
LVHW030322070526
838199LV00069B/6538